A Winning Gift

MARGUERITE HENRY'S

Ponies of Chincoteague

◆ A Winning Gift ◆

CATHERINE HAPKA

Aladdin

New York London Toronto Sydney New Delhi

ALADDIN

An imprint of Simon & Schuster Children's Publishing Division
1230 Avenue of the Americas, New York, New York 10020
This Aladdin paperback edition July 2015
Text copyright © 2015 by The Estate of Marguerite Henry
Cover illustration copyright © 2015 by Robert Papp
Also available in an Aladdin hardcover edition.
All rights reserved, including the right of reproduction in whole or in part in any form.
ALADDIN is a trademark of Simon & Schuster, Inc.,
and related logo is a registered trademark of Simon & Schuster, Inc.

For information about special discounts for bulk purchases, please contact
Simon & Schuster Special Sales at 1-866-506-1949 or business@simonandschuster.com.
The Simon & Schuster Speakers Bureau can bring authors to your live event.
For more information or to book an event contact the Simon & Schuster Speakers Bureau
at 1-866-248-3049 or visit our website at www.simonspeakers.com.
Book design by Karina Granda
The text of this book was set in Adobe Caslon Pro.
Manufactured in the United States of America 0817 OFF
4 6 8 10 9 7 5 3
Library of Congress Control Number 2015936987
ISBN 978-1-4814-3969-5 (hc)
ISBN 978-1-4814-3968-8 (pbk)
ISBN 978-1-4814-3970-1 (eBook)

· CHAPTER ·

1

"HOLD STILL, CLOUDY." MADDIE MARTINEZ tightened her grip on her pony's hoof as Cloudy tried to pull it away. "I have to finish picking out your feet, and then I have a surprise."

"What kind of surprise?" her friend Vic asked.

Vic and her twin sister, Val, were fussing over a chubby bay pony in the next set of crossties. All three girls had just finished their group riding lesson at Solano Stables. Maddie and Vic were still working on their mounts' post-ride grooming, though Val had thoroughly brushed her lesson pony, picked out all four hooves, and returned him to his stall at least ten minutes earlier.

But that was Val for you, Maddie thought fondly. She and Vic might be identical twins, with the same wavy reddish-brown hair and wide hazel eyes, but in every other way they were as different as night and day. Val was one of the most efficient and organized people Maddie knew. And Vic, well, wasn't.

"What kind of surprise?" Vic said again, sounding a little impatient.

"Chill. You'll see in a sec," Maddie told her with a laugh. She quickly finished cleaning out Cloudy's hoof, then dropped it and straightened up. "Are you almost finished with Chip? Because I'll probably need your help with this." She glanced at Val. "Both of you."

"I'm done now." Vic gave the bay pony one last swipe with her brush, then grabbed the lead rope she'd dropped on the ground by her grooming kit. "I'll take him to his stall and be back in a flash!"

As Vic hurried off, dragging Chip behind her, Val wandered over and picked up one of Maddie's brushes. She started going over Cloudy's already-immaculate palomino pinto coat.

"She's pretty clean," she said. "Aren't you going to take her back to her stall?"

"Nope. She has to be here for the surprise," Maddie told her. "You'll see."

Val looked curious, but she didn't ask any more questions. "So today's lesson was fun," she said instead.

"Every lesson is fun. Especially when I'm riding Cloudy." Maddie gave the pony a pat on the shoulder, smiling as she thought back over that day's ride. She and the twins had regular group lessons together twice a week. Usually they rode on Saturdays, but this week they'd switched to Sunday afternoon because the twins had gone to a family wedding the day before. That had actually made things a little easier for Maddie, since she hadn't needed to rush over to the barn after her Saturday-morning soccer scrimmage.

Val glanced at Maddie over Cloudy's back. "Speaking of Cloudy, did Vic tell you her latest theory?"

"I don't think so," Maddie said, instantly curious. Vic was always full of theories and ideas. And since Val sounded mildly disapproving, that meant this one was probably fun or at least interesting. "What is it?"

"She thinks your parents are going to buy Cloudy for you for your birthday." Val used her brush to flick a speck of dust from Cloudy's shoulder. "She thinks that's why they were so quick to agree to let you have your party here next weekend."

Maddie laughed. "So Vic thinks Mom and Dad are going to tie a big bow on Cloudy and give her to me? I wish! Sadly, I'm afraid Vic is delusional." She gave the pony another pat. "My parents made it pretty clear they weren't interested in pony ownership when I tried to raise money to buy Cloudy over the summer. Remember?"

"Of course *I* remember that." Val rolled her eyes. "Vic? Not so much."

"Not so much what?" Vic hurried up to them, out of breath and clutching her lead rope. "Never mind. I don't care. I want to hear about Maddie's surprise."

Maddie glanced at her. "So you think my parents are buying Cloudy, huh?" she said. "Sorry, not happening. I tried that a few months ago, remember?"

Thinking back to those days made her smile now, though it had been pretty stressful at the time. And no wonder. For a while Maddie had been sure she was going to lose Cloudy.

And that wasn't acceptable. Maddie had adored the spunky Chincoteague pony mare ever since the day Ms. Emerson, the owner of Solano Stables, had bought her. Cloudy had arrived half trained and pretty wild. Her previous owners had bought her as a weanling and had shipped her all the way from the East Coast, mostly because she looked almost identical to the pony made famous in Marguerite Henry's classic book, *Misty of Chincoteague*. They'd tried to train her but hadn't done a very good job, and by the time she was eight years old, Cloudy was way too much for them to handle.

But Ms. Emerson had seen something special in the sweet-natured pony, and so had Maddie. She'd read *Misty of Chincoteague* dozens of times and could hardly believe that a real live Chincoteague pony was right there at her barn in Northern California, an entire continent away from the tiny island where she'd been foaled.

She'd watched, fascinated, as the experienced barn owner had started Cloudy's retraining, first teaching the mare ground manners—how to walk quietly at the end of a lead rope and to pick up her feet to be cleaned or trimmed by the farrier. After that Ms. Emerson had moved on to restarting Cloudy under saddle. Those earliest rides had been pretty exciting, at least in Maddie's opinion, since all Cloudy knew how to do was take off at a high-headed gallop as soon as someone mounted. But Ms. Emerson had stayed patient, showing the pony that it was okay to walk and trot with a rider on her.

It wasn't long before Maddie started asking to ride Cloudy. At first the answer was a firm no—Maddie had been taking lessons for only a matter of months at that point, and Ms. Emerson just kept repeating her favorite saying: "Green plus green equals black-and-blue." Maddie was still green—new to riding—and so was Cloudy.

But a few weeks later, Cloudy was cantering quietly and popping over tiny jumps. Even Ms. Emerson had to admit that the mare was learning fast. Maddie might not have been the most experienced lesson rider at that point, but she was one of the boldest—and definitely the most persistent. So the barn owner had finally allowed her to try Cloudy in a lesson. They were only allowed to walk and trot in the beginning, and the first couple of rides had been pretty challenging for Maddie, since Cloudy was a lot more sensitive than the placid lesson ponies she'd been riding up to that point. Even so, she'd known as soon as she climbed into the saddle that she and Cloudy just clicked.

A year and a half later, Cloudy was one of the stable's steadiest, most reliable lesson horses—safe for any beginner, but with enough spunk left to keep things interesting when more experienced riders climbed into the saddle. Sometimes Maddie fantasized about having Cloudy all to herself— never having to share her with other lesson riders, knowing she'd always be there waiting for Maddie when she came to the barn. But that was all it had ever been. A fantasy.

Then the previous owners had turned up over the summer, wanting to buy Cloudy back. Maddie had freaked out and tried everything she could think of to stop them, including raising money to buy the mare herself—at least until she'd realized Ms. Emerson had no intention of selling Cloudy.

Maddie snapped out of her reminiscing when Vic poked her hard on the shoulder. "A few months ago it wasn't your birthday," Vic said. "Now it is."

"True." Maddie shivered with excitement. She was turning twelve in exactly one week. Her parents and Ms. Emerson had agreed to let her throw a party at the stable, and Maddie had invited more than two dozen of her closest friends. "I guess we'll have to see. But I'm not holding my breath."

"Really?" Vic sounded a little disappointed.

"Yeah." Maddie smiled at her. "It's okay, though. I'm happy with the way things are. Cloudy *almost* feels like mine, you know?"

"I can't wait for your party, Maddie." Val tossed her brush back in Maddie's grooming bucket. "It's going to be fun."

"Totally," Vic agreed. "But we can talk about that later. Surprise?"

"Oh, right." Maddie stepped over to her backpack, which she'd dropped in a corner of the grooming area. Digging inside, she pulled out a small bottle. "Check it out."

Val peered at the bottle, which sparkled in the barn's overhead lights. "Nail polish?" she said, sounding mystified. "Um . . ."

"Since when are you a nail polish kind of girl, Mads?"

Vic grabbed the bottle from Maddie. "Especially Pink Twinkle nail polish?"

Maddie glanced at her own hands. Her fingernails weren't exactly manicure ready. Between riding Cloudy, playing soccer, riding her bike, and everything else she liked to do, it was way too much trouble to do more than clip off the ragged ends now and then.

"I'm *not* a Pink Twinkle kind of girl," Maddie told the twins. "But Cloudy? She totally could be."

"Huh?" Val still looked confused. But Vic raised an eyebrow.

"Are you saying what I think you're saying?" she asked with a grin.

Maddie grinned back. "Just try to keep her still, okay?"

Squatting down beside Cloudy's front hooves, she uncapped the nail polish. Cloudy pricked her ears and looked down as the sharp smell drifted through the grooming area.

"Hold still, girl," Vic said, putting a hand on one of the crossties to steady the pony.

Maddie carefully swiped the nail polish onto Cloudy's

left front hoof, leaving a sparkly pink stripe. Val watched, still looking a bit perplexed.

"Well, now I know why you spent so much time cleaning her hooves off today after lessons," she said.

"Yeah." Vic grinned. "It looks awesome! Where'd you get the polish?"

"Tillie's dresser." Maddie added another swipe. "She's got like a zillion bottles of makeup-type goop sitting there. She probably won't even notice this one's gone."

Val watched as Maddie edged the nail polish wand down toward the bottom of the hoof. "Don't get any hay or dirt in it."

"Hay and dirt just add texture," Vic told her sister with a laugh. "Hey, Mads, I hope it lasts until your party!"

"If it doesn't, we'll just have to have another manicure session before then." Maddie sat back on her heels and surveyed the pink-glitter-covered hoof. "Gorge!"

"Totally," Vic agreed.

Even Val smiled. "Actually, it does look pretty cool."

"Cool doesn't cover it. You look *fabulous*, Cloudy!" Maddie drawled, doing her best to imitate the fashion commentators she'd seen on TV. "Pink is so definitely your color, darling."

"Definitely!" Vic and Val chorused.

Suddenly Cloudy pricked her ears, turning her head to look down the barn aisle. A second later Maddie heard the squeak of the wheelbarrow and saw the stable's newest part-time stall cleaner coming their way. He was tall and lanky, with floppy dark brown hair and a slightly crooked smile. Maddie had talked to him only a few times, enough to discover that his name was Seth, he was a freshman at the local high school, and he was working at the barn to earn some quick spending money even though he didn't know much about horses. Still, he seemed nice enough, and more important, he was intrigued by the fact that Cloudy was a Chincoteague pony—a rare breed anywhere, but especially in Northern California.

"What are you guys laughing about over here?" he asked with a friendly smile. "It's scaring the horses."

Vic stuck out her tongue at him. "Very funny!"

"Oh, it's nothing," Maddie said. "We're just giving Cloudy a manicure."

Seth glanced down at the pony's hooves, and his eyes widened. "Oh, man!" he said, snorting with laughter. "Does Ms. Emerson know you're doing that?"

"Good question." Val looked concerned. "I didn't think of that."

Maddie shrugged. "She let those little kids paint Wizard's hooves with that glitter stuff from the tack shop for the last show, remember? This is the same thing. Pretty much."

"That's our Maddie," Vic said. "Why ask permission when you can ask forgiveness instead?"

Seth laughed. "Good one." He stepped over and gave Cloudy a rub on the neck. "Hope you like pink glitter, Cloudy."

"Make sure you clean her stall extra well, okay?" Maddie told him. "She doesn't want to mess up her manicure."

"You got it." He grinned. "Speaking of which, I'd better get back to work. Later, guys."

"See you." As he walked off, Maddie returned her attention to Cloudy, scooting around to attack her other front hoof. "How about that, Cloudy? You're already turning guys' heads with your new look."

Vic glanced after Seth to make sure he was out of earshot. "And a *cute* guy, too."

Maddie shot her a smirk. "Uh-oh. Don't tell me you're going boy crazy on us!"

"You don't have to be boy crazy to notice that guy," Vic protested. "I mean, I have eyes, okay?"

"Whatever." Maddie feigned concern as she gazed at Vic. "All I know is that my friend Haley has these friends who got infected with the boy bug, and now they're totally impossible."

The twins exchanged a look. "Haley?" Val said. "She's one of your Pony Whatsit friends, right?"

"Pony Post, yeah." The Pony Post was a private website with just four members. Maddie had met the other three girls online and had bonded with them over their shared love of Chincoteague ponies. Haley Duncan lived in Wisconsin, where she competed a pony named Wings in the challenging sport of eventing. Nina Peralt owned a pony named Bay Breeze and kept him at a barn in New Orleans. Brooke Rhodes lived on Maryland's Eastern Shore, just a few miles north of Chincoteague and Assateague islands. She kept her pony, Foxy, in her rural backyard.

Even though they lived so far apart, the four girls had become fast friends since starting the website together. Maddie usually checked in with them at least once a day, sharing everything about her time at the barn with Cloudy—and the rest of her life, too.

That reminded her—she wanted to take some pictures of Cloudy's new look to share with the other Pony Posters. She quickly finished painting Cloudy's right front hoof, then fished her phone out of her bag.

"Oops," she said. "Forgot to turn this back on after our lesson."

When she clicked the power button, two new texts appeared. The first was from her older sister, Tillie:

Hey, do u have any idea what happened to
my new nail polish? B/c it was VERY VERY

$$$, and if u had something to do with
it disappearing, u will be sorry! ☹

"Uh-oh," Maddie muttered.

"What?" Vic peered at the phone over Maddie's shoulder. "Yikes! Think she's talking about the Pink Twinkle?"

"Maybe," Maddie said. "Um, probably. Okay, definitely." She glanced at the nearly empty bottle of nail polish and winced. Tillie didn't have much of a sense of humor, and Maddie knew she probably wouldn't be at all amused by what had happened to her Pink Twinkle. "I suppose that's why this one was way at the back of her makeup junk," Maddie mused aloud. "She probably didn't want Mom and Dad to notice it and guess how much she spent on it, since they keep bugging her about putting more money in her savings account for college. But whatever—I'll deal with her later."

She clicked over to the other new text. It was from her friend Bridget:

Maddie!! Text me back as soon as you
can. I need you!!!! My life is pretty
much over, and I don't know what
to do!!!!!!!! Srsly, text me back,
OK????!!?? ☹ ☹ ☹

"Uh-oh," Maddie said again. Bridget tended to be pretty dramatic, but this was extreme even for her. Maddie quickly tapped the response bar to text her back. "Better find out what this is about . . ."

✦ CHAPTER ✦
2

MADDIE LOOKED UP AS A CLATTER OF hurried footsteps rang out from the barn entrance. Bridget had just appeared in the doorway, slightly disheveled and out of breath. Even so, she still looked more stylish than most people ever did, in a brightly patterned skirt and her beloved chunky-heeled vintage sandals. Maddie had no idea how her friend could ride a bike in those shoes, but she knew better than to ask. Bridget would just make a joke about it being one of her many and varied talents.

Then again, she didn't look to be in a joking mood at the moment. Her eyes were red, and she was sniffling as she hurtled toward Maddie. Even her hair looked sad. Bridget liked to experiment with her long, straight black hair, sometimes piling it all on top of her head and stabilizing it with a sparkly clip or a pair of fancy chopsticks, and sometimes braiding it or pulling it up in a jaunty ponytail. But today it just fell loose around her shoulders and over half her face.

"OMG, Mads," Bridget exclaimed, flinging herself at Maddie. "I'm soooo upset!"

Maddie staggered back slightly, but braced herself and hugged her back. "What's wrong, Bridge?"

Bridget sniffled loudly, then pulled away. "It's about Tony. He just totally d-d-*dumped* me!"

"Oh, Bridget." Maddie wasn't sure what else to say. Tony was Bridget's boyfriend—well, ex-boyfriend now, it sounded like. The two of them had become an item at arts camp the previous summer. Even though they lived far apart, they'd stayed in touch after camp ended, trading daily texts full of hearts and other lovey-dovey emojis and weekly phone calls that Maddie could only imagine consisted mostly of dreamy sighs and kissing noises.

"I thought he was the one!" Bridget wailed, grabbing

Maddie for another hug. "I can't believe he'd do this to me!"

Maddie held back a sigh. Bridget was only a year ahead of her in school, which made her almost thirteen. How could she think she'd already found "the one"? It just didn't compute.

Still, Bridget was her friend, and Maddie hated to see her hurting. "Come on," she said, gently disentangling Bridget's arms from around her neck and grabbing her by the hand. "Vic and Val are here. They're good listeners, so you can tell us all about it and we'll try to help, okay?"

"Okay." Bridget sniffled and followed Maddie down the aisle to the grooming area.

When they got there, Val was touching up Cloudy's hooves with what was left of the Pink Twinkle, while Vic leaned against the wall and watched. They both looked up when Maddie and Bridget appeared.

"Hey, guys," Maddie said. "You remember Bridget, right? Bridge, it's Vic and Val."

"Right, hi," Bridget said vaguely. All four girls attended the same enormous public middle school, but Bridget was a grade ahead of Maddie and the twins. Bridget probably wouldn't have known Vic and Val at all if Maddie hadn't introduced them a few times at the barn. Bridget lived less than a quarter of a mile away from Solano Stables, and even though she'd never shown much interest in horses, she sometimes came to hang out with Maddie or watch her ride. Likewise, Maddie tried to attend most of Bridget's plays and art shows.

Sometimes Bridget joked that Maddie had tricked her into becoming friends by pretending to be an artsy type instead of the jock she really was. The two of them had met soon after Maddie had moved to the area three summers earlier. Her mother was career Air Force, which meant the family moved around a lot. Maddie was used to making friends fast and had immediately signed up for summer day camp as a way to meet other kids. The soccer and rock-climbing camps had been full already, so she'd ended up in a session sponsored by a local theater group. The campers had put on a production of *Alice in Wonderland*, and Bridget and Maddie had been cast as Tweedledum and Tweedledee. Ever since, they'd been the best of friends despite their differences.

"So what's wrong?" Vic asked Bridget in her straight-forward way. "You look kind of upset."

"That's an understatement!" Bridget flopped down dramatically onto a hay bale, earning a surprised snort from Cloudy. "My boyfriend just dumped me."

"They've been a couple since the summer," Maddie told the twins.

Val's eyes widened. "Wow! That's a long time."

"Four months, three weeks, and five days," Bridget announced. "But who's counting?" She sighed loudly. "I can't believe he did this to me! I thought everything was fine."

"So what did he say?" Maddie asked. "Maybe you misunderstood him or something."

"No way." Bridget sat up straighter and glared at her. "He said the long-distance thing was just too hard, and so he decided to go to the school dance next weekend with some stupid girl from his math class. Can you believe that?"

"Wow," Vic said. "That's harsh."

"I know, right?" Bridget's big brown eyes welled up. She gazed forlornly at Cloudy, who was still eyeing her curiously. "Maybe I should give up on boys, dedicate my life to my art.

Or to saving animals, or something. You know—something worthwhile. That'll show Tony he made a mistake!"

Maddie traded an uncertain look with the twins. None of them had much experience with boys yet. Not in the romantic sense, anyway. Maddie had tons of guy friends, but nobody she'd ever even slightly considered might become a boyfriend.

"Look, Bridge," she said. "You're amazing, and if Tony didn't appreciate you, maybe it's better that he set you free, you know?"

"Are you crazy?" Bridget sniffled and glared at her again. "Tony is am-am-a*maz*ing!" A single tear leaked out and trailed its way down her face.

Maddie hurried over and sat down on the hay bale beside Bridget, giving her a hug. "Don't cry," she exclaimed. "Seriously, he's not worth it."

"No boy is worth crying over," Vic added with a decisive nod.

"Yeah," Val added, though she didn't sound too sure. "Anyway, he lives pretty far away, right?"

"Utah," Bridget sobbed. "I was already trying to

convince my parents to let me go visit him there over winter break. It was going to be totally romantic."

"Look." Maddie gave her one more squeeze, then grabbed her hand and yanked her to her feet. "Whenever I'm feeling down, I just come here and hug Cloudy, and that always makes me feel better. Why don't you give it a try?"

"Cloudy?" Bridget eyed the mare dubiously. "What do you mean, hug her? How do you hug a horse?"

"Like this." Maddie demonstrated, throwing her arms around Cloudy's neck and burying her face in her mane. She breathed in deeply, enjoying the familiar scent of the warm pony. Then she stepped back and waved Bridget forward. "Go ahead—give it a try."

"I don't know." Bridget took half a step forward. "Will she bite me?"

Vic laughed. "Not unless you smell like hay."

"Don't worry," Val added. "Cloudy's really sweet. She doesn't bite."

Bridget took a deep breath and stepped even closer. "This is weird. . . ." She gingerly snaked her arms around the pony's neck, imitating what Maddie had just done. Cloudy turned her head and snuffled at the girl's hair, and Bridget leaped back with a shriek. Cloudy threw her head in the air, rolling her eyes in surprise.

"It's okay," Maddie said, trying not to laugh. "She was just saying hello."

"If you say so." Bridget smoothed down her hair, surveying the pony from a safe distance. Then she let out a long sigh. "Anyway, hugging a pony isn't like hugging your boyfriend."

"If you say so," Maddie echoed.

"It's kind of hard to hug someone who lives in Utah, isn't it?" Vic added.

Val poked her sister. "You're not helping."

But Bridget barely seemed to have heard Vic's comment. She was staring sadly into space. "Now I'll never get to hug him again." Her eyes filled with tears again. "I can't believe he did this to me!"

As she tried to figure out what to say to make her friend feel better, Maddie heard the sound of the wheelbarrow rattling toward them again. Seth was returning from his latest trip to the manure pile.

He rounded the corner, whistling. "Hi, guys," he called

when he saw them. "How's the pony manicure going?"

Bridget glanced at him and blinked rapidly several times. Then she turned away, quickly dabbing at her eyes with the sleeve of her shirt. Maddie guessed she was embarrassed to be caught crying by someone she didn't know.

"It's going great," she told Seth as he approached, trying to distract him. "Check it out. Is she ready for the Paris fashion runways or what?"

Seth laughed, stopping the wheelbarrow in front of Cloudy and reaching out to give the pony a pat on the face. "I wouldn't know about that," he said, flipping his hair out of his eyes with a toss of his head. "But she looks pretty spiffy."

"Thanks." Sneaking a look at Bridget, Maddie could see that she'd composed herself. "By the way, Seth, this is my friend Bridget. She just, uh, stopped by to say hello. Bridget, this is Seth."

"Hi, Seth." Bridget smiled at him. "Do you work here?"

Seth waved a hand at his wheelbarrow and pitchfork. "It's not glamorous, but it pays pretty well. And Ms. Emerson lets me come whenever I have time between school and football practice."

"Oh, you're on the football team?" Bridget asked. "What position do you play?"

"Quarterback," Seth replied.

Bridget's eyes widened. "Really, quarterback? Wow, that's cool!"

"Thanks." Seth smiled proudly. "I'm only JV this year, but I'm hoping to make varsity as a sophomore."

"Cool," Maddie said. "I didn't even know you played football."

"There's a lot you don't know about me." He waggled his eyebrows. "Like, you probably don't know I have a secret double life as an international spy."

Maddie laughed. "Really? What a coincidence—me too! What's the last international crisis you stopped?"

"If I told you, I'd have to kill you." Seth grinned and checked his watch. "Speaking of getting killed, I'd better go finish up. My mom will strangle me if I'm late for dinner again."

"Okay. Later." Maddie gave a quick wave as he hurried off.

When she turned back to her friends, Bridget was

smirking at her. "Where've you been hiding *him*, Mads?" she demanded.

"Huh?" Maddie glanced over her shoulder. "You mean Seth? He's just the new stall guy."

"Just the new stall guy, hmm?" Bridget said. "You two seemed awfully friendly. Is there something you want to tell me?"

"Tell you?" Maddie echoed, still not catching on.

"Yeah. Just because I don't have a boyfriend anymore doesn't mean you have to hide yours from me."

"Maddie and Seth?" Vic exclaimed. "No way."

"Yeah, what she said." Maddie rolled her eyes and patted Cloudy, who was nosing at her sleeve. "He's not my boyfriend! I barely know him."

"So you're still in the love-at-first-sight stage, huh?" Bridget grinned. "Because seriously, Maddie. It's so obvious you're crushing on him."

"It is?" Maddie was so confused that she wasn't sure how to respond. "Um . . ."

"I mean, you were just flirting your head off!" Bridget stepped closer and poked her on the shoulder. "Ooh, Seth,

I didn't know you played football," she cooed in a high voice that sounded absolutely nothing like Maddie. "What a coincidence. We have soooo much in common! Giggle, giggle!"

"I do *not* giggle," Maddie told her. "Anyway, your heartbreak has obviously gone to your head and made you insane. Because if you think that was flirting, you're nuts."

"Yeah, Maddie jokes around with everyone," Val put in. "She wasn't flirting." She glanced uncertainly at Maddie. "Were you?"

"Of course not!" Maddie said. "Seth is nice and all, but I definitely don't have a crush on him."

Bridget looked at the twins. "No wonder Maddie spends so much time here," she said. "And all this time I thought the only one she had a crush on was Cloudy! Is Seth here a lot?"

"Almost every day after school," Val replied. "There are like twenty stalls, so it usually takes him a while if he's the only one working."

"And does Maddie follow him around looking all moony?" Bridget asked.

"No," Maddie said before the twins could respond. "Give it up, Bridge. Seth's only been working here for about five minutes—I barely even know him! Besides, he's way too old for me."

The smirk was back. "The lady doth protest too much, methinks," Bridget said.

Maddie blinked at her. "Say what now?"

"It's a quote from *Hamlet*," Bridget explained. "I played Ophelia when we did a session on famous scenes from Shakespeare at camp." Her smirk faded, and her lower lip started to quiver. "Tony played Hamlet."

Uh-oh. Maddie wondered if she should have played along with the crush-on-Seth thing. At least it had distracted Bridget from her heartbreak for a few minutes.

"Um, want to go somewhere and talk about it?" she offered. "We could ride our bikes over to the diner and get sodas or something."

"Thanks. But that's okay." Bridget looked around. "I'd rather stay here."

"Are you sure?" Maddie was surprised. While Bridget didn't seem to mind visiting the barn now and then, she'd never acted as if she liked it all that much, either. Usually she ended up complaining about the smells and the way bits of hay got stuck to her clothes and hair.

"Yeah." Bridget gave her a slightly shaky smile. "It's nice here. And Cloudy is awfully cute with her sparkly hooves. Can I, you know, brush her off or something?"

"Sure!" Now Maddie was more surprised than ever. As far as she could remember, Bridget had never showed the slightest interest in interacting with Cloudy beyond a quick pat now and then. "Here—use this one." She grabbed a soft body brush and handed it over.

"Thanks." Bridget flipped her hair back over her shoulder, then cautiously touched the brush to Cloudy's shoulder.

Vic giggled. "You can press harder than that. She won't mind."

"Just act like you're brushing your own hair," Val suggested.

"Here, I'll show you." Maddie grabbed another brush and demonstrated, running it over Cloudy's side in long, sweeping motions.

She was still surprised that Bridget wanted to stay at the

barn instead of drowning her sorrows over a soda or an ice cream sundae or something. But she wasn't going to complain about it. Why sit in some boring diner when you could hang out with the coolest pony in the world instead? Being with Cloudy always made Maddie feel better when she was down. Maybe her magic was working on Bridget, too.

◆ CHAPTER ◆

3

MADDIE'S STOMACH WAS RUMBLING when she walked into her kitchen on Monday afternoon. She'd had soccer practice after school, and Coach Wu had kept them hustling the whole time. Maddie hadn't even had a spare moment to eat the granola bar she'd brought as a snack. She hadn't eaten it on the way home, either, since she'd caught a ride with one of the other players' mothers, and the woman's car was so spotless that Maddie was afraid to move, let alone eat.

Her father looked up from loading the dishwasher when Maddie walked in. "There you are," he said, not quite smiling. "I was just starting to wonder if you'd run away from home to escape the wrath of Tillie."

Maddie grimaced. "Is she here?"

"Yes, she's up in your room. And still not happy."

Maddie could tell her father wasn't particularly thrilled with her, either. By the time she'd arrived home from the barn the previous afternoon, she'd been in some serious hot water. It was hard to say how much of her parents' annoyance came from the fact that Maddie had taken something that didn't belong to her without asking—always a cardinal sin in their house—and how much was from having to listen to Tillie gripe at them about it for more than an hour before Maddie turned up. Either way, it had ended in a long lecture and lots of dirty looks from Tillie for the rest of the evening.

Not eager to face her older sister now, Maddie wandered to the fridge and looked inside. Suddenly there was a sound like a herd of thundering elephants, and her two younger brothers raced into the kitchen.

"Hey, it's Maddie!" nine-year-old Tyler exclaimed. "You're still alive! We thought for sure Tillie would have put out a hit on you by now."

Ryan didn't say anything, though he pushed his glasses up his nose and stared at Maddie curiously. He was a year older than Tyler, but much quieter. Then again, as Maddie liked to say, the average tornado was quieter than Ty and usually caused less of a commotion.

"Whatever," Maddie muttered. She couldn't believe everyone was getting so worked up over a stupid bottle of nail polish. She'd even offered to replace it with her own money—at least until she'd heard it cost almost thirty dollars.

"Thirty bucks for nail polish?" she'd exclaimed. "Who would pay that much for something you can get at the drugstore for ninety-nine cents?"

That definitely *hadn't* been the right thing to say, logical though it might have seemed. It had brought a howl of outrage from Tillie and more stern words from her parents.

Maddie's father set one last coffee mug in the top rack and turned to look at her. "So I hope it was worth it," he commented without quite meeting Maddie's eye. "I mean, I hope Pink Twinkle turned out to be a good look on Cloudy, at least."

Tyler snorted with laughter. "Good one, Dad!"

Ryan just rolled his eyes behind his glasses. Maddie smiled.

"Yeah, it looked great on her," she said. *Much better than it would have on Tillie*, she was tempted to add, but didn't quite dare. Her father might not be as strict as her military mom, but he didn't have much sympathy for any kid who did something he or she knew was wrong.

"You could finish up the leftover chicken if you're hungry," he told Maddie. "Don't spoil your appetite, though—we're eating in less than an hour."

"Okay," Maddie said meekly. "Thanks, Dad."

"Wait! Can I have some of that chicken?" Tyler asked.

His father raised his eyebrows. "Didn't you have a sandwich half an hour ago?"

"Yeah. So?"

"No chicken for you." Maddie's father hurried out of the room. He rarely stopped moving for long, whether at his part-time job as a nurse at the local hospital or while running the household while his wife was working full-time at the base. A moment later Maddie heard the basement door open and guessed he was doing laundry.

She grabbed the plate of foil-covered chicken out of the refrigerator. When she turned around, Ryan and Tyler were staring at her.

"So are you grounded?" Ryan asked. "Because Tillie says you should be locked up for the good of society."

"Tillie says a lot of things." Maddie popped a piece of chicken into her mouth. "Anyway, it's none of your business."

"Maybe you should give Tillie all your birthday presents to make it up to her," Ryan suggested.

"Yeah." Tyler grinned. "*If* you can find them. I can't believe you haven't found any yet!"

Maddie felt a spark of interest at that. In their family, it could be hard to keep a secret, and birthday gifts were no exception. Maddie's parents always hid the kids' gifts around the house, and the kids always did their very best to find them before their birthdays.

"Have you even looked?" Tyler asked.

"Sure." Maddie chewed and swallowed, then snagged another piece of chicken. "A little. I haven't had much time, what with school and soccer practice and riding. . . ."

"And stealing Tillie's valuable designer nail polish," Tyler added.

"Yeah, and that." Maddie quickly stuffed the last couple of pieces of chicken into her mouth, then stuck the plate in the dishwasher. "Look, I don't have time to stand around here all day talking to you pip-squeaks. Later."

She hurried out of the kitchen, wiping her mouth on the back of her hand. The boys' comments had reminded her that her birthday was only six days away, and she hadn't found a single gift yet. That was pathetic, and normally Maddie would have been all about making up for lost time.

But she wasn't really in the mood just then. Somehow, that kind of family tradition seemed like a lot less fun when the rest of the family was mad at her. Making a mental note to search more in a day or two, when things cooled off, she headed upstairs.

When she got there, she paused outside the door to the bedroom she shared with Tillie. The sound of a plaintive love song drifted out from behind it.

Steeling herself, Maddie pushed the door open. Tillie was sitting at her desk doing homework. She frowned when she saw Maddie.

"What do you want?" she demanded. "Let me guess— you came to steal my cashmere sweater to wipe the horse poo off your boots."

Maddie smiled weakly. "I'm not staying. I just need this." Stepping over a few piles of clothes and other stuff on her side of the room, which looked like a before picture to Tillie's tidy "after" half, she grabbed her laptop off her desk.

Soon she was perched on the window seat at the far end of the upstairs hallway. She checked her e-mail, then logged on to the Pony Post. As the logo of galloping Chincoteague ponies appeared on the screen, Maddie sighed, wishing she could be with the real thing right then. Even if everyone else seemed to be mad at her, Cloudy never held a grudge and was always ready for a hug.

But there was no way she could fit in a trip to the barn today even if her parents would have allowed it. Which they wouldn't, given the circumstances. What with how dramatic Tillie was acting about all this, Maddie considered herself lucky they'd still allowed her to go to soccer practice instead of just chaining her in the basement or something.

There were several new posts since the last time she'd logged on that morning. Maddie scanned them, her mood lifting slightly as she read.

[BROOKE] Hi all! Happy Monday! Anyone here?

[HALEY] I'm here! Hi B. Did u ride today?

[BROOKE] Not yet. I just got home from school a little while ago. I was thinking about skipping riding today b/c it's soooo cold out! But I think I'll have some hot cocoa and then at least hop on bareback for a few min. What about u?

[HALEY] Nope. Wings has the day off today. We don't usually ride on Mondays. But tomorrow if it doesn't snow too hard, we'll be back to work.

[BROOKE] Snow? Brr! And I

thought it was cold here!!!

[HALEY] LOL, it'll prolly just be flurries. If

it's not too windy I'll ride anyway. B/c guess

what? I decided I want to be ready to enter

a real recognized event in the spring.

[BROOKE] Rly? Cool! I'm sure you'll be ready

by spring. U have been learning a lot lately,

right? Esp. in that clinic u did last month.

[HALEY] Def! That's what gave me the idea.

I've been thinking about it ever since then. But

after our great rides this weekend, I decided for

sure. I even know which event I want to enter.

It's the first one of the spring around here, and

it's at the same farm where I did the clinic.

[BROOKE] That's good. U and Wings

will already know yr way around.

Oops! Mom just got home and has
a car full of groceries to unload, so
gtg—will check in later if I can. . . .

[NINA] Hi all! Anyone still on?

[NINA] Guess not. Oh well! But, Haley,
that's fab news! A recog. event is a big
deal, right? I know you and W will do great
tho, b/c you're just that awesome!!

[NINA] Also, I'm posting some pix from
my trail ride today. Don't be jealous, B,
but it was pretty hot here, so we kept it
short. We also kept it short b/c my friend
Jordan's bro came with us again. He's
becoming a pretty good trail rider!

[BROOKE] Hey, Nina. Sorry I missed
u earlier! Great photos! Is that Brett?
He's just as cute as u said, lol!

[BROOKE] Oh, almost forgot—I didn't ride this afternoon after all. Boo! My little brother saw some dumb old cowboy movie last week, and now he thinks he's the Lone Ranger or something. He's been bugging me to go for a ride on Foxy, and today my mom made me let him. Of course, my little sis hates being left out, so she wanted a turn too. Foxy was an angel—I think she was confused by those little monsters bouncing around up there, lol! She was good as gold. But by the time the twins finally got bored and went inside, it was getting too dark to ride. Oh well. There's always tomorrow. . . .

Maddie smiled as she read over her friends' adventures. It was cool to know that she had friends all over the country doing interesting stuff with their ponies at the same time she was having fun with hers.

She only wished she had some riding stories of her own to report that day. But her friends would just have to settle for updates on her news from yesterday. She'd filled them in the night before about the nail polish thing and also about Bridget's breakup.

She opened a new text box and started to type.

[MADDIE] Hi guys! Great pix, Nina! Brooke, where are the pix from Foxy's pony ride? Lol! If your little sibs ride again, better let us see! Anyway, bummer that u didn't get to ride, but actually, I think it would be kinda cool if any of my siblings showed any interest whatsoever in ponies or riding. Well, except maybe Tillie—at least not right now . . . Needless to say she's still furious about the Pink Twinkle incident. My parents aren't exactly thrilled with me, either. I just hope they all get over it before Sunday, or my b'day party is gonna be pretty grim!!! Speaking of grimness, Bridget moped around school all day—at least, whenever I saw her, she looked pretty mopey. I wish I knew how to help her feel better, you know? I mean, it doesn't

seem worth it to get so worked up over some

boy anyway, but what do I know? Lol! I guess

all I can do is be a friend and be here for her.

She sent the post and then signed off. Noticing that her laptop battery was low, she glanced at her bedroom door at the opposite end of the hall.

"Better not plug it in in there," she muttered. "I don't want Tillie to decide to throw it out the window to get back at me."

Okay, so Tillie wouldn't really do that. Probably. Even so, Maddie wasn't in the mood to face her sister again until she absolutely had to, so she headed back downstairs. The boys were in the den playing their favorite car-racing video game.

"Where's Dad?" Maddie asked.

Ryan didn't even glance up from the screen. But Tyler looked her way briefly.

"Basement," he muttered. Then he bent over his joystick again.

Maddie glanced at the door to her parents' home office, which was located only steps from the den. She was tempted to go in and plug in her laptop without asking. She was sure her dad would say yes anyway.

But she didn't quite dare, especially right now, when she was already in the doghouse. The home office was her parents' domain even more than their bedroom. All four kids were strictly prohibited from going in there without permission, since her parents kept lots of important documents in there, along with the computer her mother used when she worked from home.

So Maddie headed down the hall past the kitchen and stuck her head through the basement door. "Dad?" she called down the stairs. "Can I plug my computer in in the office?"

"Sure, go ahead." His voice floated back up. "But don't touch anything else."

"I know. I won't."

She hurried back to the office and slipped inside. It was cool and dim in there, with blinds covering the windows and everything neat and tidy.

Well, almost everything. As Maddie set her laptop on the desk by the charger, she noticed that one of the drawers was slightly ajar.

"Better close it or Dad will think I was snooping," she muttered.

She reached for the drawer, then hesitated. What if her parents had gotten smart and started hiding birthday gifts in here? None of the kids dared poke around in the office—it was the perfect hiding place!

I'm not snooping, she told herself as she bent a little closer to the drawer. *I'm not going to open it any further. Can I help it if I accidentally happen to see what's in there?*

There were no boxes or wrapping paper in the drawer, though. In fact, it was almost empty. The only thing Maddie saw in there was a piece of paper with a bunch of printing on it and the official US Air Force seal at the top.

"Work stuff," she murmured. "Boring."

She was about to shut the drawer when a surprising word caught her eye: "London." Was her mother taking a business trip overseas? That hadn't happened in a while, and Maddie couldn't help being curious.

Bending closer again, she scanned the page—and let out a gasp. The paper said that the Air Force had officially approved six plane tickets to London in January.

Six tickets. London. January. Maddie stared at the words, stunned. Had her mother been transferred again? Could the family really be moving to England—in just a little more than two months?

◆ CHAPTER ◆

4

MADDIE SAT IN THE NOISY SCHOOL CAFE-
teria on Tuesday, staring into space. All around her, kids
were eating and laughing and talking and goofing off, the
volume of the place only slightly less than that of a jet taking off at the Air Force base. But all Maddie could focus
on was that piece of paper she'd seen yesterday.

She hadn't said anything to her family about it, of
course. How could she? If she did, they'd know she'd been
snooping in the office, and that would have been a risky
thing to admit even if she wasn't already in trouble. She'd
been lucky to get off with a warning and a loss of allowance
on the nail polish thing; if she admitted she'd been poking

around in the forbidden zone, it was likely to end with some much more serious punishment. Maybe even her birthday party getting canceled.

Besides, if she told them and they said it was true? Well, that would be that. She wouldn't be able to pretend it had all been her imagination.

Even though she already knew it totally wasn't . . .

"Maddie! Earth to Maddie!" Bridget snapped her fingers in Maddie's face.

Maddie blinked and glanced up as her friend set down her tray. The scent of the cafeteria's mystery meat wafted across the table. "Oh, sorry. Hi," Maddie said.

"Hi." Bridget sighed loudly and plopped down onto the seat across from her. Since the two of them were in different grades, lunch was the only time they saw each other during the school day other than occasionally passing in the halls. "What's up?"

"Not much," Maddie said automatically. Then she paused, tempted to tell Bridget what she'd discovered. After all, she was one of her best friends. Maybe she could help her figure out how to deal with this. So far Maddie hadn't breathed a word to anyone, not even Vic and Val. The twins were in a different section from Maddie this year, so she saw even less of them than she did of Bridget. They even had lunch at a different time.

"So I just keep thinking about him, you know?" Bridget said, poking at her lunch with her fork. "Everything reminds me of him. Every time my social studies teacher mentions medieval England, I remember how Tony used to yell 'bring out your dead!' all the time." At Maddie's mystified look, she added, "It's a quote from some old movie he really likes." She sighed again. "And every time I see a guy walking around with his sneakers untied, I think it's him for a second." She picked up a forkful of peas and stared at them. "Even this stupid lunch reminds me of him! He used to text me funny pictures of his lunch after his friends built things with it."

"Built things?" Maddie echoed.

"Yeah." Bridget smiled wanly. "Like, they'd pile up all their Salisbury steaks to make a fort and sculpt ninjas and stuff out of the mashed potatoes. He's, like, really artistic, you know?"

Maddie took a sip of her milk. "Yeah, you're always saying he's really, um, creative." In her opinion, Tony had always sounded pretty immature, and Bridget was probably better off without him. Not that she could see that right now. "Just try not to dwell, okay? It'll get better."

"Maybe." Bridget shot her a pathetic look. "Hey, are you going to the stable today after school?"

"I was going to, yeah," Maddie said. "But I can hang out with you instead if you need me."

"I do," Bridget said. "But actually, I was hoping I could come to the stable with you."

"You were?" Maddie was a little surprised. Sure, Bridget had seemed to enjoy herself the other day. But Bridget almost always enjoyed something new and different. She tended to get bored pretty easily after that.

"Yeah." Bridget dropped her fork and reached for her water bottle. "It's so nice and busy and homey, you know? And nothing there reminds me of, you know, you-know-who." She wrinkled her nose, then sighed and looked sad again.

"Sure, no problem." Maddie reached across the table

to pat Bridget's hand. "You can come to the barn with me anytime."

"Thanks." Bridget's lower lip quivered slightly. "I really appreciate you being here for me, Mads. It makes me feel less alone."

Maddie forced a smile. Okay, maybe it wasn't the best time to tell Bridget she might be leaving soon—for a whole other country.

"So who else is around today?" Bridget asked as she and Maddie stepped into Solano Stables that afternoon. "Do you have, like, a riding lesson or something?"

"Not today, no." Maddie paused and took a deep breath of the hay-and-horse-scented air, instantly feeling less anxious about the whole moving-to-London thing. Or at least ready to forget about it for a while. Then she led the way down the aisle toward Cloudy's stall. "Vic and Val won't be here this afternoon," she told Bridget. "They have music lessons on Tuesdays."

"Really? What kind of music lessons?"

"Vic plays the saxophone, and Val—" Maddie began.

"Hi!" Bridget blurted out suddenly, cutting her off. When Maddie turned around, her friend was staring into one of the stalls they'd just passed.

"Hey," a friendly voice responded. A second later Seth stepped into view, pitchfork in hand. He wiped his brow with the back of one hand. "You guys just can't stay away from this place, huh?"

Bridget laughed. "Look who's talking!"

"They pay me to be here," Seth joked. "What's your excuse?"

Bridget smiled and shot a look at Maddie. "Oh, I'm sure that's not the *only* reason you like it here, right?"

Maddie gulped, suddenly nervous. Bridget was always friendly, so it was no surprise she'd stopped to say hello when she'd noticed Seth. But maybe she was getting a little *too* friendly. What if she said something to Seth about her ridiculous theory that Maddie liked him? "Gotta go, Seth," she said quickly. "We were just on our way to see Cloudy." She grabbed Bridget by the arm, trying to drag her off.

But Bridget's feet were planted in place. "Have you

cleaned Cloudy's stall yet?" she asked Seth. "If not, we could take her out and, you know, groom her or whatever. So she's not in your way?"

"Thanks," Seth said. "Actually, I already did hers, though."

"Oh well." Bridget shot Maddie another mischievous look. "Maybe next time."

Okay, Maddie was really getting anxious now. Bridget could be kind of unpredictable—she was almost impossible to embarrass and found it amusing to try to embarrass her friends sometimes. Normally Maddie was pretty tough to embarrass, but she definitely didn't want Seth to get the wrong idea. Talk about awkward!

"Hey, I just had an idea," she blurted out. "Let's ask Ms. Emerson if you can go for a ride!"

"Huh?" That distracted Bridget from Seth. "But I don't know how to ride—you know that. I've never even been on a horse before in my life!"

"I know, but it'll be fun. We can do a pony ride."

Bridget looked dubious. "Okay, so that means I'll be closer to the ground when I fall off?"

Maddie laughed. "No. I don't just mean you'll be riding a pony, though you will be, since I figured we'd use Cloudy. A pony ride means I'll lead you around so you don't have to steer or anything. It'll be a piece of cake!"

"Yeah, you should do it," Seth put in, still listening. "I went on a pony ride when I first started here, and it was cool."

"Really?" Bridget smiled at him uncertainly. "Well . . ."

Maddie grabbed her arm again, and this time Bridget allowed herself to be dragged away. "Come on. Let's go ask Ms. E."

They found the barn owner in the feed room supervising a grain delivery. When she heard Maddie's idea, she looked Bridget up and down and then nodded. "That should be fine," she said. "Cloudy isn't on the schedule for any lessons today, so it'll be nice for her to stretch her legs. You can borrow one of the lesson helmets from the tack room, Bridget."

The two girls headed back out into the aisle. "What did she mean, it would be nice for Cloudy to stretch her legs?" Bridget sounded nervous. "We're not going to gallop or anything, right?"

"No, she won't get to stretch them *that* much." Maddie chuckled and led the way down the aisle to the tack room. "It's just that Solano Stables doesn't have much room for pastures and stuff, since land is so expensive around here. So the horses here don't get to spend a lot of time grazing and running around in big fields like they do in other places."

"Oh," Bridget said. She watched as Maddie grabbed Cloudy's saddle and bridle off their racks, along with a clean saddle pad.

"Yeah, like where my friend Haley lives, for instance," Maddie went on as she eyed Bridget's head and then grabbed a helmet off the shelf of spares that Ms. Emerson kept for lesson students who didn't have their own. Jamming it onto Bridget's head, she nodded with satisfaction and then headed for the door, still talking. "Haley's family's farm has, like, acres and acres of pasture, since they have cows and stuff. So her pony, Wings, gets tons of turnout time. And then there's Brooke—she has a pasture in her backyard. It's not huge, but it's all for her pony, Foxy, who lives outside twenty-four-seven, pretty much."

"Got it." Bridget was starting to sound a little bored.

"At least we have a few decent-sized paddocks here. That's more turnout than there is at Nina's barn," Maddie said. "She lives right in the middle of New Orleans, and her pony's boarding barn is in this big city park with practically no space for grazing at all."

By then they'd reached Cloudy's stall. Maddie handed the saddle and bridle to Bridget, then opened the stall door. The mare was nibbling at her hay, but she lifted her head when the girls stepped inside.

"Hi there, cutie," Bridget said. "You're not going to try to kill me, are you? Good girl!"

Maddie laughed. "Don't worry. She's great at taking care of nervous beginners. You'll be fine."

Clipping a lead rope onto Cloudy's halter, she led the pony to the grooming area. As she attached the crossties, Seth passed by, pushing his wheelbarrow.

"So the pony ride is on?" he asked.

"Yeah," Bridget said, yanking the helmet off her head and smoothing down her hair. "I just hope I survive!"

He laughed. "You'll do great. Maddie seems like she'd be a good teacher."

"Hmm." Bridget glanced at Maddie. "Yeah, Mads is good at a lot of stuff. Don't you think so?"

"Okay," Maddie said loudly, not wanting to let that line of discussion go any further. "Let's get Cloudy groomed and tacked up now. You can brush her if you want."

Seth wandered off as the two girls set to work getting the pony ready. A few minutes later Maddie was leading Cloudy toward the outdoor riding ring, with a progressively more nervous looking Bridget trailing along beside her.

"Are you sure this thing will work if I fall off?" she asked, fiddling with the chin strap of her borrowed helmet.

"Sure. But you won't fall." Maddie gave Cloudy a pat. "Cloudy won't let you. This one time, a beginner was riding her in a show and lost her balance after a jump. Before she could tip off the side, Cloudy scooted over and got under her again. She was fine—ended up getting a ribbon in the class and everything."

"Jumping?" Bridget looked alarmed. "We're not doing that today, are we?"

Maddie laughed. "No jumping, don't worry. We'll just walk around, maybe try a trot if you want."

There was nobody in the ring, so Maddie swung open the gate and led Cloudy in. Bridget followed, carefully closing the gate behind her.

"Maybe you should ride instead," she suggested. "I could just watch."

"Nope, this is all you." Maddie positioned Cloudy beside the wooden mounting block. The pony stood quietly, occasionally swishing her tail at a late-season fly.

Bridget surveyed her with anxious brown eyes. "She looks taller all of a sudden," she said. "Did I ever mention I'm scared of heights?"

"You are not." Maddie grinned at her. "You even went hang gliding with your grandpa once, remember? Now climb up on the mounting block. I'll make sure she stands still while you get on. Just put your right hand on the back of the saddle and grab a handful of mane with your left hand."

"What? Grab her hair?"

"Don't worry. It won't hurt her." Maddie forgot sometimes that not everyone knew those kinds of things. "She won't even notice. Once you're ready, put your left foot in the stirrup and swing up and over."

Bridget took a deep breath and nodded. "Okay. Here goes nothing. . . ."

She was actually pretty graceful getting on, catching her weight on her hands and lowering herself carefully into the saddle instead of plopping down like most beginners did at first.

"Great job," Maddie said. "All those years of dance classes are paying off, I guess."

Bridget smiled tightly. "Don't let her move yet, okay?" she said, scrabbling for the reins. "I'm not ready."

"Don't pull too hard," Maddie warned as Bridget shortened her reins so far that Cloudy lifted her head in surprise.

"Sorry." Bridget loosened the reins a fraction of an inch. "I want to be able to stop her if she runs away."

"I know most people think you stop a pony with the reins, but that's not really true," Maddie said. "I mean, yeah, most horses are trained to slow down or stop if you pull back. But if they really want to go, you can pull as hard as you can and they won't stop."

Bridget's eyes widened in alarm. "Oh, great!" she exclaimed. "Let me off this thing!"

"No, wait, sorry," Maddie said. "Cloudy isn't going to run away like that."

"Are you sure?" Bridget countered. "Come to think of it, I saw her run away with you once. Why didn't I remember that before I agreed to this?"

For a second Maddie didn't know what she was talking about. Then she remembered—once when Bridget had come to watch a lesson, Cloudy had taken offense to Maddie's attempts to get her to leg yield and had jumped into a canter instead, shaking her head and being silly.

"That wasn't running away," she said. "Anyway, she never does stuff like that with beginners. Or anyone who's nervous, even. She's really smart." She patted the mare on the neck. "Aren't you, Cloudy?"

"Okay." Bridget sounded a little dubious. "Still, I don't want to totally let go of the reins. You know, just in case."

"You don't have to," Maddie said. "I'm just saying, you don't have to keep them quite so tight, okay?"

Leaving one hand on Cloudy's bridle—more to comfort Bridget than for any other reason, since the pony was standing quietly—she tugged at the reins until Bridget let them slide out to a reasonable length.

"Okay, now I'm going to walk her forward," Maddie said. "Try to relax and go with the motion."

"Easy for you to say," Bridget muttered.

As Cloudy moved off at a slow amble, Bridget let out a squeak of alarm and hunched forward. "Sit up straight," Maddie said.

"But I feel like I'm going to fall off!" Bridget protested.

Maddie shrugged. "You don't look like you're going to fall off."

That was true. As Maddie had mentioned, Bridget had taken dance classes for years. Her hips were automatically following the pony's movement, even though her upper body still looked tense.

Maddie knew that if Bridget would just relax, she'd have a better time. But how could she get through to her?

Suddenly she had an idea. "Hey, remember when you were telling me about the breathing exercises you learned in that acting class you took last spring?" she said. "You said they really helped with stage fright."

"They did," Bridget agreed. "I used them a lot at camp last summer."

"Okay," Maddie said quickly, not wanting to get sidetracked by *that* particular topic—and the particular boy it was likely to bring up. "Why don't you try some of those exercises now?"

"Huh? Are you kidding?" Bridget sounded confused. "I'm riding a horse, not getting ready to go onstage."

"Hey, how's it going out here?"

Maddie turned and saw Seth standing in the doorway watching them. He hurried forward and leaned on the ring fence.

"Hi," Maddie greeted him, glad that Bridget was too distracted to be likely to mess around and tell him anything embarrassing. "She's a little nervous."

"Yeah, this is totally terrifying," Bridget called to him. "But I'm going to try some breathing exercises I learned in acting class."

"You're an actor?" He looked impressed. "Cool!"

Bridget just smiled. Then she closed her eyes briefly. Maddie could hear her counting under her breath.

She just waited, keeping Cloudy wandering around the ring at a slow walk. They were only a little over halfway around when Bridget stopped counting.

"Hey, it worked," she said. "I feel more relaxed already. I think I may even be getting the hang of this riding thing!"

Maddie smiled. Bridget did look more relaxed. "Maybe you just needed an audience," she joked, nodding toward Seth. "You are an actress, after all."

Both Bridget and Seth laughed at that. "Maybe," Bridget agreed.

"Looking good up there!" Seth called. "Are you going to try a trot?"

"Don't pressure her," Maddie warned him. "She's just getting the hang of walking."

"No, he's right," Bridget said. "I think I'm ready. Can we trot now?"

Maddie was surprised, but she had to admit that her friend looked pretty solid up there now that she'd settled down. Her body was following the motion of Cloudy's walk, and her hands had relaxed on the reins. She was sitting up straight and looking where she was going. Even Ms.

Emerson would probably agree that she was ready.

"Okay," she said. "Cloudy's trot is really smooth, but it'll probably still feel kind of weird. Just keep your heels down and try to absorb the movement in your back. If you start to bounce too much, you can stand up in the stirrups and hold on to her mane."

"Got it." Bridget nodded. "Let's do it."

Maddie clucked and gave a little tug on the rein she was holding. "Trot, Cloudy," she said. "Trrrrot!"

At the same time, she broke into a jog herself. The pony started trotting, almost surging past Maddie.

"Easy, girl," Maddie said, tightening her grip on the rein to let Cloudy know that she didn't need to go so fast.

Then she glanced back at Bridget, a little worried that her friend might have been thrown off balance by the sudden transition. But Bridget was still in position. Not only that, but she actually appeared to be posting—rising and falling with the rhythm of the pony's gait—even though Maddie hadn't told her about that yet!

"Is this okay?" Bridget asked. "It feels right, and it sort of looks like what I've seen you do when she trots."

"Yes." Maddie smiled, proud of her friend. "It's totally all right. Bridget, you're a riding genius!"

Bridget giggled a bit breathlessly. "Thanks! I have a good teacher." She smiled at Seth as they trotted past him. "Isn't Maddie the best?"

He laughed. "Sure! Have fun." With a wave, he headed back inside.

Bridget made Maddie trot her around the ring one more time before they stopped. "That was cool," she said, all smiles as she leaned forward to pat Cloudy on the neck. "Now I sort of see why you spend so much time doing this."

"Yeah." Maddie smiled back, glad that she'd helped take her friend's mind off her troubles.

Come to think of it, she'd pretty much forgotten about her own problem for a while, too. Now it came rushing back as she looked at Cloudy and imagined moving a whole ocean away from her.

Glancing up at Bridget, she was tempted to spill what she'd seen in that office drawer. But Bridget looked so happy that Maddie didn't want to spoil the nice moment. Telling her about the move would just have to wait.

◆ CHAPTER ◆
5

AS SOON AS SHE OPENED HER EYES ON Wednesday morning, Maddie reached for her laptop. Maybe she didn't feel right telling Bridget about her problem yet. But that didn't mean she had to keep it to herself. She'd poured out the whole story to the Pony Post last night right before she went to bed.

None of the other members had been on the site at the time, which wasn't surprising. When it was nine o'clock at Maddie's house in California, it was already eleven p.m. in Wisconsin and New Orleans and midnight in Maryland. But that also meant all her friends woke up before she did, so Maddie guessed she'd have some responses by now.

Sure enough, when she logged on, there were new posts from all three of her friends.

[BROOKE] Oh wow, M, I'm so sorry! I can't believe this! Are you sure about what u saw? What did your parents say when u asked them about it? Is the move definite, or is there any possibility it might not happen?

[HALEY] OMG I can't believe this!!! London???? Wow. Exciting in a way—but how can they expect u to leave Cloudy behind??????

[NINA] Ack! H is right. London is amazing, but making you leave Cloudy behind is cruel and unusual punishment for sure!!

Despite her worries, Maddie smiled at Nina's "cruel and unusual punishment" comment. Nina's dad was a successful attorney, and clearly some of that had rubbed off on her. Maddie wondered if she could hire Mr. Peralt to sue her parents for ruining her life. She was sure no jury in the world could possibly vote against her, especially if she was allowed to bring Cloudy into the courtroom. She let her eyes flutter shut for a moment as she imagined the scene. Cloudy would have to dress properly for court, of course—maybe in a nice pantsuit. . . .

Then Tillie bustled into the room, freshly showered and wrapped in a towel. "Are you ever going to get up?" she griped, shooting Maddie the evil eye. "Because I need to be at school early today, and I won't be happy if I'm late because you're lounging around like a slug all morning."

Maddie didn't think that was particularly fair, especially since the alarm hadn't even gone off yet. But it didn't seem worth a fight.

"I'm up," she assured her sister, sitting up a little straighter. Then she scanned Nina's second post.

[NINA] But you can't just give in, girl! You have to fight this. We'll help in any way we can. Let's all start thinking, OK, girls? Mads, let us know more when you can and we'll be there!

Maddie smiled again at that. She really did have the greatest friends in the world!

And hey, at least when it comes to the Pony Post things won't change between us whether I'm here or way off in England, she thought. *It'll just mean a bigger time difference, that's all.*

That made her feel a tiny bit better. But only until she glanced at the photos on the site, including the latest ones she'd posted of Cloudy a few days earlier. Sure, she could stay in touch with her human friends and make new ones wherever she went. She was good at that. What she wasn't good at? Imagining her life without Cloudy in it.

She bit her lip, trying not to dwell on that. Tillie was over at her dresser, humming as she dabbed perfume on her wrists. Maddie wrinkled her nose at the sickly sweet smell, then bent over her keyboard and started typing a response.

[MADDIE] Hi guys. Thanks for the sympathy. To answer ur question, B, I haven't talked to my parents about this yet. Like I said yesterday, I saw the news when I was snooping in their office, which is totally forbidden. And as u know, they're already mad at me for the Pink

Twinkle thing, so I don't want to push it. Esp.

with my b'day only 4 days away now. If it's my

last one at Solano Stables, I def. don't want

to ruin it!! KWIM? But I'll try to find out more

soon and let u know. Tx again. Luv u all!!!

She posted the message and sat back, reading over her friends' messages one more time. Suddenly a rolled-up sock hit her in the head.

"I'm serious," Tillie snarled. "If you make me late for school today, you're dead meat."

"Fine, I'm up." Clicking the Pony Post shut, Maddie sighed and rolled out of bed, knowing that the next thing Tillie threw at her was likely to be a lot heavier. Normally she'd take that sort of thing as a challenge, but today she just wasn't in the mood.

Maddie's mood got even worse when she walked into math class and saw the teacher holding a stack of papers.

"Ugh. I hardly had time to study for this stupid quiz,"

mumbled one of her classmates, a guy named Brick, who was on Maddie's summer community soccer team.

Maddie grimaced. "If you studied at all, you're in better shape than me. I totally forgot."

The teacher had announced the quiz yesterday. Maddie remembered that now. At the time, she hadn't paid much attention—she'd been more focused on fretting over the London thing. Then, in the afternoon, she and Bridget had been having so much fun at the barn that they'd stayed until dinnertime, and well . . .

"Bummer." Brick shot her a look. "But you're smart, Martinez—you'll do fine."

Maddie crossed her fingers as the teacher handed out the papers, hoping Brick was right. But as soon as she scanned the first few questions, she knew she was in trouble.

"Hey!" Bridget hurried up to Maddie's locker. "You going to the barn today?"

Maddie looked up from trying to shove her science book into her already-crowded locker. Pushing a strand of dark hair out of her face, she nodded.

"I'm going," she said. "And believe me, I really need some pony time today."

Bridget peered at her. "Is something wrong? You look cranky."

"I *am* cranky." Maddie finally got the book in. Slamming the door shut before the other books could decide to stage an escape, she turned to face her friend. "I'm pretty sure I blew my math quiz today."

"Really?" Bridget didn't sound very interested. "Well, it's just one quiz, right?"

"Tell that to my parents." Maddie rolled her eyes. "Every quiz is like the SATs to them."

Bridget laughed. "And people call *me* dramatic? Seriously, Mads, your grades are great. Especially in math, right? Your parents aren't going to freak out over one bad quiz."

Maddie just shrugged, not bothering to argue. Besides, maybe Bridget was right. Oh, not about Maddie's parents—they were complete and utter freaks when it came to grades.

But maybe this time it didn't matter so much. After all, she'd be leaving this school very soon. And who knew what her classes in England would be like. Did they even have the same kind of math over there? Probably not, since they did everything in pounds instead of dollars and meters instead of yards.

"What?" Bridget leaned closer, peering into her face again. "Are you sure it's just a quiz that's bothering you? You look really weird."

Maddie opened her mouth, tempted once more to tell her friend what was going on. Then she shut her mouth again and shook her head.

"I'm fine," she said. "Like I said, I'm just craving some Cloudy time."

"Cool. So can I tag along again?" Bridget fell into step beside Maddie as she headed down the hall.

"Sure, I guess." Maddie glanced at her. "Today's my group lesson with Vic and Val, though. So there might not be time for a pony ride."

"A group lesson?" Bridget looked intrigued. "Do you have to be, you know, pretty experienced to be in that?"

"Not really," Maddie said. "Ms. Emerson believes in mixing different levels together in group lessons whenever she can. That way the less experienced riders can watch the better ones and—wait a minute. Why are you asking?"

Bridget grinned and shrugged. "My ride on Cloudy was fun yesterday. I was thinking maybe I should learn more about riding." She poked Maddie in the arm. "Not that you're not a fabulous teacher. But a real lesson could be cool."

"No, it's okay." Maddie's foul mood drifted away, and she started grinning, hardly daring to believe what she was hearing. "Ms. Emerson is a way better teacher than me. So wait, are you serious? You want to join our lesson?"

"If you don't mind."

"Mind? Are you crazy?" Maddie laughed. "I've only been telling you for a year and a half how much fun riding is! Of course I'm psyched that you're finally catching on!"

"Cool." Bridget looked pleased. "And check it out—I even wore boots today."

She stopped and waggled one foot, which was encased in a stylish suede calf-high boot. Maddie smiled, though now that the surprise was wearing off, she was starting to feel slightly queasy. It was super-amazing that one of her best friends had discovered the joy of riding—thanks to the most wonderful pony in the world, of course. It would be fun having Bridget around the barn, showing her the ropes and watching her bond with Cloudy and the other ponies.

At least for the next couple of months. Because according to what Maddie had seen in that desk drawer, they'd have only until January to ride together. After that, who knew if they'd ever see each other again. At least not more than once a year or so when Maddie flew back for a visit . . .

But Maddie shook her head, suddenly fed up with feeling gloomy all the time. That wasn't her. If she had only a couple of months to watch Bridget fall for horses and riding, then she wanted to enjoy every second of it while she could.

She linked her arm through Bridget's. "Let's go," she said with a grin. "This is going to be fun."

Ms. Emerson seemed a little surprised to see Bridget again. But after a quick phone call to Bridget's mother, she agreed that she could ride in the lesson as long as Vic and Val didn't object.

"That's totally fine," Vic said when Maddie and Bridget found her in the grooming area and asked. "It'll be fun having someone new in the group."

Val nodded, glancing up from brushing her pony's fetlocks. "Me too," she said. "It's fine. Who are you going to ride today, Bridget?"

"Oh." Bridget shot Maddie a look. "Uh, Cloudy, I guess?"

Maddie blinked. Somehow she hadn't even thought about which pony Bridget would ride. It made sense that she'd expect it to be Cloudy, since Cloudy was the only pony she'd ever ridden. But Maddie hadn't been on her favorite pony since Sunday, and given what had happened since then, she really needed some Cloudy time herself right now.

"Um," she said. "We should probably ask Ms. E. Stay here. I'll go."

She dashed off down the aisle, leaving Bridget chatting with Vic and Val. Ms. Emerson was in the barn office, going over some paperwork.

"Hey, who should Bridget ride?" Maddie blurted out. "Like, maybe Wizard, right?"

Ms. Emerson looked up. "Doesn't she want to stick with Cloudy?"

"Oh. Um, she thinks she's too fast, maybe?" Maddie

shrugged. "I don't know. She liked the look of Wiz, though."

That wasn't entirely untrue, she told herself. The two girls had wandered through the barn yesterday, giving treats to all the horses and ponies, and Bridget had commented on Wizard's sweet brown eyes and silky white mane.

"All right. In that case, Wizard is fine," Ms. Emerson said. "You'll help her groom and tack, yes?"

"Absolutely." Maddie grinned and tossed the barn owner a sloppy salute that would have made her mother's commanding officer swear. "Thanks, Ms. E."

She returned to the grooming area. Seth had appeared while Maddie was gone, accompanied by his wheelbarrow and pitchfork.

Maddie nodded a quick hello at Seth, not even looking directly at him. She figured Bridget was probably distracted by the lesson thing, but you never knew. "Hey, Bridge, Ms. E says you should ride Wizard. He's the cute little gray pony you met yesterday, remember?"

"What?" Bridget looked alarmed. "But I thought I'd get to ride Cloudy again. You said she's the best with beginners."

"Wiz is great at that, too," Vic put in. "He's super-quiet."

"But—" Bridget began.

"Seriously, Vic's right," Maddie said quickly. "Wizard is the calmest horse in the entire barn. He'd sooner fall asleep than run away with you."

Val giggled. "I'm not sure he knows how to run."

"Aw, don't be dissing the Wiz-man!" Seth put in with a grin. "He's the coolest."

Bridget blinked, turning toward him. "Really?"

"Yeah." Seth leaned on his pitchfork. "He's my favorite." Glancing at the two ponies the twins were getting ready, he added, "No offense, other horses."

"Hmm." Bridget looked thoughtful. "I guess if you're sure Wizard will be okay . . ."

"I'm sure," Maddie told her, relieved. Bridget could be stubborn, and when she got stubborn, she also tended to get dramatic. And Maddie didn't feel like dealing with that today. "Come on. I'll help you get him ready."

Fifteen minutes later, Maddie was slipping the bridle over Cloudy's ears. "Ready to go, baby girl?" she whispered as she buckled the noseband and throatlatch.

She'd already helped Bridget get Wizard ready, leaving

the two of them standing by the ring with Vic and Val while she raced to get her own mount tacked up. Pulling the reins over Cloudy's head, she gave a cluck.

"Let's go, Cloudy," she said. "Don't want to be late."

They hurried through the barn and out the back. Vic and Val were already mounted and walking their ponies around on the rail. Ms. Emerson was holding Wizard by the mounting block. Bridget was standing on the block, looking nervous.

Maddie held her breath, watching as her friend swung aboard the stout gray pony. "Good," Ms. Emerson said. "Pick up your reins, and I'll double-check your girth. . . ."

Maddie let out her breath as Ms. Emerson continued talking to Bridget, explaining the proper way to hold the reins and telling her a little bit about Wizard. Leading Cloudy into the ring, she waited until they'd moved away from the block, then checked her girth and mounted.

She settled into the saddle, smiling at the familiar feel of Cloudy beneath her. "Let's go, girl." She clucked and gave the faintest squeeze with her legs to move the pony away from the mounting block.

Ms. Emerson was walking beside Wizard. When she

saw that Maddie was ready, she stopped the quiet gray pony and called for attention.

"As you all know, this is Bridget," she said. "Since she's new, we'll take it easy and stick with a lot of walking for our warm-up."

"Oh." Bridget blushed beneath her borrowed helmet. "Are you sure? You don't have to change everything you usually do just because I'm here."

"It's fine." Ms. Emerson shot her a quick smile. "It's good for all riders to revisit the basics now and then. There's a lot one can do at the walk. For instance, we'll start by doing windmills. Maddie, can you demonstrate for Bridget, please? Right arm first."

Maddie immediately shifted both reins to her left hand. Then she stuck her right arm up and started swinging it around in a big circle. The twins did the same, keeping their ponies walking along the rail at the same time.

"Okay, now you try, Bridget," Ms. Emerson said. "I'll lead the pony so you don't have to worry about steering just yet."

Bridget imitated what the others were doing. "Like

this?" She giggled. "This is fun! It's sort of like an acting exercise we do to loosen up."

"Exactly." Ms. Emerson smiled. "It does the same thing in this case, plus it helps you find your balance in the saddle. All right, now we'll switch to the other arm. . . ."

As the lesson continued, Maddie could tell that Bridget was having fun. She was having fun, too. They stuck to a walk for quite a while, and she could tell that Cloudy was getting a little impatient with the slow pace. But Maddie knew it was good for both of them to do something different, as Ms. Emerson had said.

They ran through a variety of exercises similar to the windmill one. Then Ms. Emerson started teaching Bridget to steer with her reins and legs by having her follow the other ponies. That went pretty well, and by the end of the last figure eight, Bridget was grinning.

"This is kind of fun," she said after bringing Wizard to a halt.

"You're a natural," Maddie told her.

Bridget smiled. "I don't know about that. But it's amazing how my dance training is coming in handy."

"Yes, it is," Ms. Emerson agreed. "You have excellent balance and body awareness, which are both very useful in riding as well as in dance. Do you think you'd like to try a short trot now?"

Bridget's smile faded, a nervous expression taking its place. "A trot?"

"She did great at trotting yesterday," Maddie told Ms. Emerson. "She just started posting like she'd been doing it forever!"

"Really?" Vic sounded envious. "It took me about a million years to catch on to posting properly."

"Me too," Val put in. "I still pick up the wrong diagonal sometimes and have to switch."

"Diagonal?" Bridget looked mystified.

"Never mind that right now," Ms. Emerson said. "Let's talk about the trot. . . ."

She went on to describe the gait and give Bridget some tips on riding it. She also had all four girls demonstrate the proper position for a posting trot—also known as a rising trot—at the halt and walk. Then she asked if Bridget was ready to move on to trotting.

"I'm not sure." Bridget bit her lip and shot a worried look toward Maddie. "Maddie led Cloudy around yesterday. Can we start out doing it that way?"

"I suppose so." Ms. Emerson put her hand on Wizard's reins. "Go ahead, you three—I want to see you trot halfway around in two point, then go to rising trot."

Maddie nodded, nudging Cloudy into a brisk trot. She stood in her stirrups, keeping her weight out of the saddle as the pony settled into the faster gait. At the same time, she glanced back over her shoulder at Bridget.

Ms. Emerson was urging Wizard into a trot. Unlike Cloudy, the little gray pony preferred to keep things as slow as possible. But after a moment, he let out a groan and broke into a lumbering trot.

Maddie could see her friend bouncing around in the saddle. "Oh!" Bridget exclaimed. "He feels a lot different from Cloudy."

"That's true," Maddie murmured under her breath. She'd ridden Wizard herself a number of times. Even though his trot was slower than Cloudy's, it was a lot bouncier.

"Up, down, up, down," Ms. Emerson said. "That's it—find the rhythm."

"This is hard!" Bridget's face was turning red with effort. But she eventually figured out how to rise and fall with the pony's gait.

"Good!" Ms. Emerson said. "Now I'm going to let go, okay? Just close your legs when you sit to keep him moving."

"Wait!" Bridget exclaimed.

But the teacher was already backing away. Wizard's gait faltered.

"Squeeze with your legs!" Ms. Emerson called.

Bridget looked panicky. "He's going too fast!" she exclaimed, hunching forward and yanking back on the reins.

That brought Wizard to an abrupt halt. Maddie gasped as she saw Bridget wobble and her foot slip out of the stirrup.

"Sit up!" she cried. "Hold on!"

It was too late. With a cry of dismay, Bridget tumbled off over Wizard's shoulder.

✦ CHAPTER ✦

6

"HOLD STILL!" MS. EMERSON ORDERED, rushing over. "Don't try to move yet."

"Ow!" Bridget wailed, rolling over and rubbing her hip, which had hit the ground first.

Ms. Emerson kneeled beside her as Wizard wandered off to nibble at the grass growing under the fence line at the edge of the ring. Maddie jumped off Cloudy and went over to grab Wizard's dangling reins. Once she had both ponies in hand, she looked over at Bridget again. She wanted to call out to her, ask if she was okay. But she forced herself to stay quiet and let Ms. Emerson handle it.

When the barn owner was convinced that Bridget

wasn't injured and hadn't hit her head, she let her climb to her feet. "All right, you got your first fall out of the way early," she said with a wry smile. "Ready to get back on the horse and try again?"

"No." Bridget's eyes filled with tears. "What if it happens again?"

Maddie led the ponies closer. "It'll be okay," she assured Bridget. "You need to get back on, or you'll just get more scared."

"I don't know if that's possible," Bridget informed her. "Maybe riding isn't for me after all."

Vic and Val had stopped their ponies a short distance away. "I know how you feel," Vic called out. "I was totally freaked out the first time I fell off."

"She was," Val agreed. "Come to think of it, she fell off Wizard that time, too."

"Yeah, but only because I got distracted and tried to turn around to look at something right when he picked up a canter," Vic said.

Maddie smiled. "See? It's no big deal," she told Bridget. "Everyone falls off sometimes."

"Especially if they're riding Wizard, it sounds like." Bridget frowned at the gray pony, who appeared to be falling asleep where he was standing. She shifted her gaze to Cloudy. "I knew I should've ridden Cloudy today!"

Ms. Emerson looked confused. Oops. Maddie decided she'd better distract her before she started asking questions.

"Maybe we should switch," she suggested. "I could ride Wizard for the rest of the lesson, and Bridge can get on Cloudy."

Bridget looked dubious, but then she shrugged. "I guess that would be okay."

Ms. Emerson looked dubious, too. "Well, normally I'd want you to get back on the pony you fell from," she told Bridget. "But since the fall happened during your very first lesson, and since you rode Cloudy successfully yesterday, I suppose we can make an exception."

"Really?" Bridget looked happier already, though still anxious as well. "Thanks!"

Maddie felt a pang of regret as she handed Cloudy's reins to Ms. Emerson. That was one more ride she'd miss.

One more out of how many? She tried not to count the days until the date on those plane tickets. . . .

Soon she was walking around on Wizard, watching as Ms. Emerson coaxed Bridget into Cloudy's saddle. Bridget looked nervous, but the barn owner stayed at the pony's head and talked her through a few circles at the walk and then a brief trot.

"Okay, that was fine," Bridget said as Cloudy came to a halt after the trot. "I think it's enough for me today."

"Are you sure?" Ms. Emerson looked surprised. "I was going to set up some poles to help you practice steering."

"Maybe next time." Bridget's tone was firm. "I don't want to do any more today."

Maddie bit her lip as she watched her friend slide down from the saddle. She was tempted to ask to switch back to Cloudy, but she felt too guilty to bring it up. After all, if she'd let Bridget ride Cloudy from the start, the fall almost certainly wouldn't have happened.

"Maddie! Heads up!" Ms. Emerson said sharply. "I said please pick up a trot—rising on the long side, sitting on the short."

"Oops." Maddie quickly gathered up her reins, realizing the twins' ponies were already trotting. "Come on, Wiz. Let's do this."

The next morning, Maddie shoveled a spoonful of cereal into her mouth and then pulled out her cell phone.

"Hey! No texting at the breakfast table!" Tyler said. He and Ryan were sitting across from Maddie, gobbling down blueberry granola bars and chocolate milk. Their father had already left for an early shift at the hospital, which meant all four kids were responsible for finding their own breakfast that day. Tillie had solved the problem by convincing her boyfriend-of-the-week to pick her up early to go out for waffles at the local diner. Normally Maddie would have tried to wheedle her way into tagging along, but today she was just glad to have Tillie out of the house.

"Says who?" Maddie mumbled in the general direction of her brother, already tapping in Bridget's name.

U are still coming to the barn today, right? she texted.

After yesterday's lesson, Bridget had seemed a little

more cheerful than Maddie had expected. She'd hung out in the grooming area, joking around with the twins and Seth, who'd stopped by to ask how Wizard had done. After the others left, Maddie had made her promise to return the next afternoon for another pony ride on Cloudy. Bridget had hesitated for only a moment before agreeing.

Maddie just hoped she wouldn't back out once she thought about it—or once the bruise on her hip started to hurt. But Bridget texted her back a moment later.

Don't worry. I won't chicken out, lol.

Maddie smiled. OK. See u at school, she texted back.

As she slipped the phone into her pocket, her mother hurried into the kitchen dressed for work. "You kids almost ready?" she asked, checking her watch. "I'll drop you off a little early. I need to stop at the bakery on my way to the base and put in the order for your cake."

"Cake?" Ryan looked up from his milk. "What kind are you getting, Maddie?"

"I'm not sure." Maddie glanced at her mother. "Chocolate?"

"What else?" Her mother winked, then grabbed a coffee thermos from the top of the refrigerator and started filling it from the pot Maddie's father had left.

"Maybe you should have a carrot cake instead," Ryan said. "Get it? Horses like carrots, right?"

Tyler wrinkled his nose. "I still can't believe you're having your party at the barn. That's weird."

"No weirder than the ninja party you had last year," Maddie countered. But her heart wasn't really in it. She'd been looking forward to celebrating her birthday at the barn. But now she wasn't sure it was such a good idea. How was she going to act normal at her party when she knew she'd be leaving soon? Especially when it was going to be at the very place she'd miss the most?

I should just talk to Mom and Dad already, she told herself, glancing at her mother's back as she poured the coffee. *Admit that I know and find out more about what's going to happen. Maybe that'll help me deal with it.*

It seemed like a good idea, at least in theory. In practice? Not so much—not right now, anyway. Her mom was in a rush, and her dad wasn't even home.

No, now definitely wasn't the time. Maddie was relieved as she realized that particular awkward conversation would just have to wait.

"Ready?" Maddie tightened the girth on Cloudy's saddle, then stepped back and brushed off her hands.

Bridget was slowly running a brush over the mare's rump. "Not quite yet," she said. "I want to clean off this spot."

Maddie stepped around to look. "Silly—that's one of *her* spots," she said. "Not dirt."

"Oh. Um, then, I guess I'm ready." Bridget glanced around the quiet stable.

Maddie followed her gaze, relishing the unusual quiet. A gaggle of adult lesson riders had just been finishing their post-ride grooming when the two girls had arrived, and now that they'd cleared out, the place was practically deserted. There were no other lessons scheduled for more than an hour. Vic and Val had other after-school activities that day. Ms. Emerson was busy in the office. Even Seth hadn't arrived yet.

"Great. Let's go." Maddie quickly bridled Cloudy and led her down the aisle.

"Wait. I forgot to get a helmet," Bridget said as they stepped outside. "Stay here. I remember where they are."

She dashed back into the barn. Maddie led Cloudy over to a patch of grass and let her graze, enjoying the feel of the pale November sun on her face.

This is nice, she thought. *Just me and Cloudy.*

Suddenly she felt tears filling her eyes. That was weird—Maddie hardly ever cried. Even when a big midfielder had crashed into her at soccer practice a couple of years ago and snapped her wrist, she hadn't shed a single tear.

But the thought of leaving Cloudy was much worse than a broken bone. Bones healed, and life went on. But moving away from her favorite pony? Maddie wasn't sure she'd ever recover from that.

"Dramatic much?" she muttered under her breath. "Bridget must be rubbing off on me."

Realizing her friend was taking an awfully long time finding a helmet, she tugged on the reins and led Cloudy back over to the doorway. Peering in, she saw Bridget ambling slowly along the aisle, pausing to glance into the stalls she was passing.

"Stop sightseeing and hurry up!" Maddie called. "We want to have time to get your ride in before the next lesson starts."

"Okay, okay." Bridget picked up the pace. "I don't have to trot today, do I?"

"Not if you don't want to," Maddie promised. "Let's just see how it goes, okay?"

She stood Cloudy next to the mounting block, and soon Bridget was in the saddle. She fiddled with the reins, glancing toward the barn now and then.

"What are you looking for?" Maddie asked.

"Nothing," Bridget said. "Just checking to make sure the lesson people aren't coming."

Maddie pulled out her cell phone to check the time. "Don't worry. We've got like half an hour before they even get here to start tacking up. Now, come on. Let's start by walking around the ring, nice and easy. . . ."

They circled the ring several times. At first Bridget was tense, leaning forward and clutching the reins tighter every time Cloudy flicked an ear or swished her tail at a fly. But after a couple of circuits she seemed to relax.

"Want to try a trot now?" Maddie asked.

Bridget frowned. "I don't know. Maybe we should wait until next time."

"Come on," Maddie wheedled. "It'll be fun. You did great the other day, remember? Anyway, it'll come in handy to know how to do it. You know—in case you ever have to ride a horse for an acting role."

That made Bridget smile. "True. I read about this actress who got cast as a runaway princess, and she was supposed to gallop out of the castle bareback on her favorite white horse."

"Actually, there aren't any true white horses," Maddie said. "Other than albinos, maybe—I'm not sure. Horses and ponies that look white—like Wizard, for instance—are actually just very pale gray."

"Thanks, Professor." Bridget rolled her eyes. "Anyway, this actress was supposed to ride off into the sunset on her *gray* horse. . . ." She paused and made a funny face. "But she kept sliding off the side of the horse. So they had to have a stunt person do it, and they just filmed her face and used special effects to paste it on the stunt person's body."

"Cool." Maddie shot her a look. "Ready to trot now? Let's go!"

She clucked and urged Cloudy forward. The pony immediately swept into a smooth trot.

Bridget let out a squeal of protest. "Hey, I wasn't ready!" she exclaimed.

Maddie grinned up at her as she jogged alongside Cloudy. "You look ready to me."

Bridget was posting, just as she had the other two times she'd ridden Cloudy. She frowned as she realized that herself. Then she shrugged.

"I guess you were right all along," she said, breaking into a big grin. "Cloudy is magic!"

The rest of the ride was fun. By the time she dismounted, Bridget was all smiles.

"That was great," she said as they headed back into the barn. "I totally didn't think about Tony at all that whole time! Partly because I was, you know, afraid of dying at first." She laughed. "But mostly because it was fun. Can we do it again tomorrow?"

"Tomorrow?" Maddie echoed. "Are you sure you want to ride again tomorrow?"

"Definitely." Bridget shot her a look. "Unless you don't want me here, hmm? Looking for some alone time with your boyfriend, and I'm cramping your style?" She waggled her eyebrows and smirked.

Maddie winced. She'd started to think that Bridget had forgotten about the whole Maddie-likes-Seth theory. Obviously not.

"Very funny," she said, glancing up and down the aisle to make sure the stall cleaner wasn't nearby.

"Look, there he is." Bridget stared toward the main entrance.

Turning, Maddie saw Seth wandering toward them, a backpack slung over one shoulder. "Hey, it's the pony girls," he greeted them in his usual friendly way. "What's up?"

"Not much, except you missed our ride," Bridget informed him. "Maddie was a brilliant teacher, as usual."

"Cool." Seth shifted his bag farther up his shoulder. "I'm late today—football practice ran long. Better get to work. Catch you later."

"Bye!" Bridget sang out as he hurried away.

"See you," Maddie added, relieved that he wasn't sticking around to give Bridget the opportunity to try to embarrass her. "So anyway," she said, turning to face her friend, "about tomorrow—I have an idea. How about if we ride together this time? Wouldn't that be fun? I can take Cloudy, and you could try one of the other ponies. Maybe Chip? He's the sweet little guy Vic rode in the lesson yesterday."

Bridget looked alarmed. "You mean the one who kept trying to pull the reins out of her hands? No thank you. I'd better stick to Cloudy—you know, at least until I'm feeling more confident. Is that okay?"

Maddie hesitated again. Normally she wouldn't have minded sharing Cloudy with anyone who seemed to need her. Especially a good friend like Bridget. But things weren't normal right then.

I need Cloudy too, she thought. *Especially since I might not have her much longer.*

Bridget peered at her. "Mads? Is that okay? It's just that tomorrow is Friday, and that was always date night for Tony and me." She stared wistfully into space. "You know—we'd talk on the phone, pretend we were together. . . ."

Maddie shook off her resentment. How could she be so selfish? Cloudy was helping Bridget get over her heartbreak, and that was the most important thing right now. It was just lucky that forcing her friend to ride a different pony hadn't totally put her off riding. If she needed to stick with Cloudy for a few more days to get her mojo back? Well, Maddie would just have to deal.

"Of course it's okay," she assured Bridget. "Tomorrow it is."

◆ CHAPTER ◆
7

[NINA] Hi, everyone! How's it going, Mads? Anything new to report? I'm still thinking about how to help; will keep u posted! Off to the barn now. Will check in later . . .

[HALEY] Hope you're having a fun ride, N! I just came in from a ride myself. Wings was great, but I was a little distracted b/c of what Maddie told us. Did u talk to your parents yet, M? Let us know what they say. Is there any chance they'd let you stay with friends to at least finish the school yr or something? That would give u a little more time with Cloudy.

[BROOKE] Hi! I'm here too—hi, Haley!

[HALEY] Hi! I hope Maddie checks in soon.

[BROOKE] She's prob at the barn spending all the time she can w/ Cloudy. I know that's what I'd be doing if I were in her shoes. Hang in there, Maddie! We will help if we can!!!

[HALEY] Def!!!! Hey, B, did u ride today?

[BROOKE] Only for a few min. My little sibs are still on their cowboy kick. They both followed me out to the barn when I went to check Foxy's water and pestered me until I gave them another pony ride. Argh!

[HALEY] Lol, sounds cute! Post more pix, OK?

Anyway, I'd better go—almost time to set the table for dinner. Check in when u can, Maddie! Bye, B!

[BROOKE] Bye!

[NINA] Hi again! I'm back—sry so late, but we went out to eat. Mmm, oysters! I'm stuffed. Anyway, Maddie, I'm hoping u check in soon—it should be like 7 o'clock there, so you may still be eating dinner. . . .

As she read Nina's post, Maddie checked the clock by her bed. It was 7:05. She opened a text box and typed quickly:

[MADDIE] I'm here! Nina, r u still on?

She posted it, then sat back and waited. It was only a few seconds before the response came:

[NINA] I'm here! Glad u are too!!!!

[NINA] How are you holding up?

[MADDIE] Ugh, I dunno. I just keep thinking about it. Jan. is sooo soon, you know?

[NINA] Ya. Did u talk to the 'rents?

[MADDIE] Not yet. It never seems to be the right time. Plus, I'm still afraid they'll be so mad I snooped that they'll cancel my party.

[NINA] I hear you. Are you maybe also afraid that if they say it's true, that will mean it's real?

[MADDIE] LOL. I already knew u were smart, N. But I didn't know u were a mind reader, too! I'm totally afraid of that!

[NINA] I would be too. No mind rdg required, lol! But ur not going to give up, are you? Maybe there's still a way to change their minds.

[MADDIE] Doubtful. The USAF doesn't

change its mind very often. When they

say u need to move, u move—kwim?

[NINA] Well, what about Haley's idea to stay

behind when they go? Maybe u could move in

w/ yr friend Bridget, or those girls from yr barn,

or??? U have tons of friends, right? I knew a

girl here who stayed w/ her cousins when her

mom had to work overseas for six months.

[MADDIE] Six months is one thing. This is prolly

supposed to be for longer than that. Anyway,

none of my relatives live anywhere nearby,

so moving in w/ them won't help. And I doubt

my parents would let me stay w/ friends.

[MADDIE] Sry. Not trying to be

negative! I know ur trying to help.

[NINA] It's OK. I understand! I hope

u at least are getting lots of quality
Cloudy time in to help u thru.

[MADDIE] Not rly. Bridget has been riding
her so much I've barely been on her. She's
coming to the barn again tmw, actually.

[NINA] Huh? But u need ur Cloudy time!!

[MADDIE] I know, but what can
I do? B needs her too.

[NINA] But if she knows what u are going
thru, she must see that she has to share!?

[NINA] Wait—don't tell me u haven't
told her about the move?

[MADDIE] I haven't told anyone
here. Just you guys.

[NINA] Hmm. Well, maybe u need to tell Bridget soon? She's a good friend—I'm sure she will understand, right?

[MADDIE] I dunno. She can be kinda emotional, u know? She will prolly freak out if she knows I'm moving away that soon. Not sure I'm ready to deal with that, kwim?

[NINA] Sure. Just think about it, OK? U need support from yr friends right now—all of them. Including Cloudy! Anyway, I'm beat. Gotta get to bed or I'll be dead in school tmw. But I will keep thinking about ways to help—promise!

[MADDIE] Thanks. Nighty-night!

After she posted her last message, Maddie sat back with a sigh. She was in her room, sitting cross-legged on her bed. Tillie was still downstairs, since it was her turn to help clear the table, which had given Maddie a few minutes of peace to check the Pony Post. She scanned the latest postings again, still impressed by the way Nina had nailed the real reason she was afraid to talk to her parents.

She's amazing, Maddie thought. *They all are. They've never let me down before—we've never let one another down. They helped me when I thought Cloudy might be sold. We helped Brooke when she felt out of place at camp. We even helped Nina when she thought she was being haunted!* She sighed and touched the Pony Post logo on the screen. *I'm just not sure it's possible for them to help with this particular problem. . . .*

The bedroom door slammed open, startling Maddie so much that she almost dropped her laptop. Tillie stalked in and glared at her.

"I have an idea," she said. "Why don't you ask Mom and Dad to trade in whatever they got you for your birthday for another bottle of that nail polish you stole from me? Then you can give it back."

"Whatever." Maddie closed the computer and stood up, not in the mood for more of Tillie's snide comments and dirty looks. "You should probably see someone about your unhealthy obsession with makeup."

She hurried out of the room to Tillie's outraged howl, yanking the door shut behind her. Then she wandered down the hall, still thinking about her conversation with Nina. As understanding as she was, Maddie could tell she didn't quite get why she hadn't told Bridget about the move yet.

Then again, that was no surprise. Maddie didn't quite get it herself. Bridget was already pretty emotional about her break-up—a little more freaking out wouldn't make that much difference. Maybe Nina was right; maybe Maddie should tell her.

Who knows? Maybe she'd even let me ride Cloudy for a change, she thought with a grimace.

Realizing she was right outside her parents' bedroom, Maddie stopped and glanced in through the half-open door. Flashing back to Tillie's mention of birthday gifts, she took a step inside and glanced around. Maybe searching for her gifts would take her mind off things for a while.

She hurried over to one of the dressers and started opening drawers, carefully poking through her parents' clothes. There were no gifts inside, but she did find something else among her father's socks.

"What's this?" she murmured, pulling out a glossy brochure.

Her eyes widened when she took in the photo of a nice-looking bay horse on the front—and the British flag. It was an advertisement for riding in London!

Heart pounding, she shoved the brochure back where she'd found it and backed away. Obviously, her parents had been researching ways that Maddie could keep riding after they moved to England. They were probably hoping that would make her okay with the move, make her forget all about Cloudy. Didn't they realize that was never going to happen? Maddie would never be okay with leaving her favorite pony behind. *Never.*

Feeling almost as emotional as Bridget all of a sudden, she hurried out of the room and looked around to make sure nobody had seen her. The hall was empty, though a moment later Tillie emerged from their room and made a beeline for the bathroom. Hearing the sound of the shower turning on, Maddie scooted through the bedroom door.

She flopped onto her bed, staring up at the ceiling. She'd never loved moving that much, but before this it hadn't seemed like all that big a deal either. Sure, a new home meant leaving old friends behind and getting used to a whole new place. But she could keep in touch with friends, and the getting-used-to part was kind of fun—like an adventure. And what could be more of an adventure than getting the chance to live in a whole new country? How many kids Maddie's age got to do that? Normally she would have been all over it.

But this time it was different. She wasn't just leaving behind people and places. Now there was Cloudy to consider too. And Maddie wasn't ready to leave her behind. Not even close.

She closed her eyes, trying to figure out how to deal with this. Because she was pretty sure she wasn't going to be able to change her parents' minds about moving—let alone the US Air Force. And she was almost as certain that her parents weren't going to let her stay behind, live with Bridget's family, or move into the spare room at Vic and Val's house. Besides, she wasn't sure she wanted that herself. She'd miss Cloudy like crazy if she left, but she'd miss her family even more if she stayed.

Opening her eyes, she sighed, feeling a bleak sense of acceptance settle into the pit of her stomach. She was moving away, leaving Cloudy behind, and that was that. She might as well figure out a way to start accepting reality.

Then she sat up, realizing there might be a tiny sliver of a silver lining she hadn't thought about. Namely, Bridget.

She's so into riding all of a sudden, Maddie thought. *And she loves Cloudy. If I have to leave, maybe Bridget can be Cloudy's new special person! That way she'll be able to keep me posted on how she's doing and send lots of pictures. And I'll know Cloudy is being pampered like she deserves.*

The thought made her feel both sad and a little bit excited. It could be kind of fun to spend the next two months teaching Bridget everything she knew about ponies in general and Cloudy in particular. She could spend every spare moment before she left with the two of them, bonding and creating lots of new memories to help her through the move.

Who knows, she thought, glancing at her well-worn copy of *Misty of Chincoteague*, which was peeking out from its usual spot on the lower shelf of her bedside table. *Maybe Bridget will even join the Pony Post!*

✦ CHAPTER ✦

8

"EW." BRIDGET PEERED INTO CLOUDY'S stall and wrinkled her nose. "There's an awful lot of pony poop in here."

Maddie glanced down as she clipped a lead rope to Cloudy's halter. There was only one manure pile in the bedding that she could see. "Are you kidding?" she said. "This is nothing."

Bridget shrugged, stepping back out of the way as Maddie led the pony out of the stall. "I'm just saying, Seth better step it up or he'll lose his job." She glanced up and down the aisle. "Where is he, anyway? I should tell him how dirty Cloudy's stall is so he can clean it while I'm riding.

We don't want her to have to go back in a filthy stall."

Maddie smiled, touched that Bridget was so concerned about Cloudy already. That would make her new plan easy to execute.

"He's probably not here yet," she said. "I think he usually has football right after school. But don't worry—if he hasn't gotten around to it by the time we finish, we can pick out the stall ourselves. I'll show you how."

"Oh. Um, okay." Bridget looked less than thrilled at that idea.

But Maddie didn't worry about it. She'd been dubious about the whole idea of cleaning up manure when she'd started riding too. But it hadn't taken long before the task was second nature.

"All right. Let's get started," she said, heading for the grooming area. "Since you're getting more serious about riding, I think it's time for you to learn how to get your pony ready."

"What do you mean?" Bridget said. "I've been helping you brush her off and stuff."

"Yeah, but that's the easy part." Maddie waved at the

pony's saddle and bridle, which they'd brought to the grooming area before going to get Cloudy. "Today you start learning how to tack up." She grabbed a hoof pick out of her grooming bucket. "But first a lesson on picking out feet."

Bridget shot a nervous look at Cloudy's hooves. "I don't know," she said. "What if she kicks me?"

"She won't." Maddie stepped to Cloudy's left front hoof. "She's already trained to pick up her feet when you grab her fetlock—that's this part of her leg here, see?"

She demonstrated, squeezing the pony's fetlock. Cloudy promptly lifted the leg, and Maddie dislodged some bedding from her foot with the pick. Then she set the foot down and straightened up, smiling at Bridget.

"See? It's easy. Why don't you try doing the other foot?" she said.

Bridget shook her head. "I don't think so," she said. "I'll help with the saddle or whatever if you want, but I'm not in the mood to get trampled today."

"You won't get trampled. She's cross-tied, remember?" Maddie tugged lightly on the tie between one side of Cloudy's halter and the wall. "She's not going anywhere."

"Still." Bridget pulled out her phone. "I've got to check my e-mail anyway. I'll be back in a sec." She stepped away before Maddie could protest, bending over her phone.

Maddie swallowed a sigh. Okay, so far Bridget wasn't making this easy. For a second she was tempted to tell her friend why she wanted her to learn everything about taking care of Cloudy—and why she needed to learn it fast.

But she decided it wouldn't hurt to keep quiet a little longer. At least until after her birthday. There was still enough time.

Maddie finished picking out Cloudy's hooves, then moved on to brushing her. Eventually Bridget wandered back and picked up a currycomb.

"I can help with this part," she said with a smile. "It's fun—like working at the pony beauty parlor."

Maddie laughed. "Yeah. Or like doing hair and makeup for one of your plays, right?"

"Speaking of makeup," Bridget said, "is Tillie still mad at you?"

"Don't ask." Maddie rolled her eyes. "But yeah, she's still pretty much not talking to me except to tell me what a loser I am. Can you believe it? Luckily, Mom and Dad seem to be over it, though."

"That's good." Bridget ran her brush slowly down Cloudy's shoulder.

Maddie flicked some dust off the pony's rump, then tossed her brush aside. "She's pretty clean," she said. "Let's move on to saddling."

"Wait," Bridget protested. "Aren't we going to brush her mane and tail? I thought maybe we could even try braiding them. I saw pictures of a cute pony all braided up online."

Maddie glanced at Cloudy's mane. "I don't usually mess with her mane and tail unless they're tangled or something. And we only braid for shows." She shrugged. "But maybe we can try it later if you want. Right now, let's get moving so you can ride, okay? Now, first you need a saddle pad. . . ."

"Whoa, what's the big rush?" Bridget stepped back as Maddie tossed a pad onto Cloudy's back. "This is supposed to be fun and relaxing, right? Anyway, I just realized—I've been spending all this time here this week, and you haven't even showed me where your party is going to be!"

Maddie straightened the pad and reached for the

saddle. "I can show you that after your ride."

"But then we'll be busy getting the saddle off and grooming her again and stuff." Bridget tilted her head and smiled. "Come on. Cloudy will be okay standing here for a minute, right? Let's go check out party central."

Maddie frowned slightly. Was it her imagination, or was Bridget acting as if she wasn't even that eager to ride? Whenever Maddie came to the barn, she couldn't wait to get in the saddle.

Then again, different people wanted different things from their time with ponies. The Pony Post should have taught her that. For instance, Haley seemed happiest when she and Wings were attacking a tough cross-country jump or other riding challenge. Maddie got that—she was the same way even if she and Cloudy didn't jump as high or gallop as fast.

Then there was Brooke, who seemed to get the most enjoyment out of teaching her pony something new and seeing her get it. She'd bought Foxy as a weanling and had been the one to do most of her training over the past four years. Maddie wasn't sure she'd have the patience for that herself, but she admired her friend for turning Foxy into a pony safe enough for her little brother and sister to ride.

Nina's pony, Bay Breeze, had come fully trained, and Nina didn't seem to mind that one bit. And while the two of them had just competed in a show, Nina had seemed more interested in coming up with a cool idea for the costume class than in winning blue ribbons. Her favorite part of riding was social—hanging out with her pony and her friends and having a good time. Riding was part of that, of course, but not the only part. Maybe not even the most important part. Now that she thought about it, Maddie guessed that Nina's version of pony time probably came closest to the way Bridget looked at her new hobby.

"Okay," Maddie said, mentally thanking her Pony Post friends for helping her to see things through Bridget's eyes. "Let's go check out party central."

She led Bridget to the addition at the back of the barn. It was a big square area with stalls along one side, but the other side was open; that was where Ms. Emerson stored the tractor and other large equipment, behind a rail meant to keep horses and ponies from getting into it. The barn owner was planning to move the equipment outside and take down the rail, leaving a roomy open space where Maddie could set up her party.

"Cool," Bridget said, surveying the area. "This will look great all decorated. What are you doing for music?"

"I already did a playlist on my phone," Maddie said. "I've got a speaker that should make it loud enough."

"Can I see?" When Maddie handed over her phone, Bridget flicked through her song selections and made a few requests.

They talked about party plans for a few more minutes before Maddie sneaked a look at the time. "We should probably go back," she said. "Cloudy's a good girl, but Ms. Emerson doesn't like us to leave horses unattended in the crossties for more than a few minutes."

"Oh, okay." Bridget followed her back up the aisle to the grooming area.

When they arrived, they found Seth feeding the pony a carrot. "Hey," he said. "I was wondering who abandoned Cloudy."

"Sorry. That was us." Bridget giggled and hurried

forward to pat the pony's nose. "Sorry, Cloudy! We didn't forget you. I promise."

"Right," Maddie said. "Okay, time to tack up."

This time Bridget didn't protest, so Maddie straightened the pad still sitting on the pony's back and then grabbed the saddle. "Uh-oh, time to go to work, Cloudy," Seth joked.

Bridget laughed again. "Don't worry. It's just a pony ride," she said. "I won't work you too hard, Cloudy." She shot a look at Seth. "Probably way less hard than your football coach makes you guys work, right?"

"Tell me about it!" Seth rolled his eyes. "I thought he was trying to kill us today."

"Okay," Maddie broke in. "Watch what I'm doing, Bridge. You need to lift the saddle up and set it gently on her back—like this. Make sure the pad doesn't get knocked out of position while you do it."

"Mm-hmm," Bridget responded, not seeming too interested. "So, Seth, how'd you get into football?"

He shrugged. "Runs in the family, I guess. My dad played in college."

"Cool." Bridget smiled at him. "Did you know Maddie's,

like, a soccer genius? She even got scouted for this really prestigious traveling team last summer."

"I didn't end up doing it, though." Maddie was starting to feel uncomfortable. She wasn't interested in making Seth her boyfriend, and she wished Bridget would stop praising her to him every chance she got. "Okay, pay attention, Bridge. I'm going to put on the girth now."

Bridget glanced over for about half a second before returning her attention to Seth. "I played soccer for one summer when I was little," she told him, still stroking Cloudy's nose. "But I was totally hopeless! I decided I'd better stick to things I was good at—like acting and singing and dancing and art and stuff."

"Wow. You do all that?" Seth looked impressed. "I can't even draw a stick figure."

Maddie sighed as Bridget laughed and started talking animatedly about the last art show she'd entered. She wasn't paying any attention at all to what Maddie was doing. Then again, at least she wasn't trying to convince Seth how wonderful Maddie was anymore.

As Maddie was buckling the noseband on Cloudy's

bridle, Ms. Emerson appeared. "Seth! There you are," the barn owner said briskly. "Can you help me with something?"

"Sure," Seth said, following her off down the aisle.

Good. Maddie quickly finished with the bridle, then led Cloudy into the aisle. "Come on," she called to Bridget over her shoulder. "Let's get you on this pony."

She expected Bridget to be more enthusiastic once she was in the saddle. And she was—for maybe five minutes. After walking around the ring a couple of times, Maddie suggested a trot.

"That's okay," Bridget said. "My legs were a little sore after my last ride. I probably shouldn't push it today."

"What?" Maddie blinked at her. "You mean you're getting off already?"

Bridget shrugged. "I have a dance recital in a couple of weeks. I don't want to be too sore to rehearse."

"Oh." Maddie wanted to argue. Bridget was going to have to get more serious about riding if she was going to take over with Cloudy once Maddie left.

But just then she spotted a couple of middle-aged women coming out of the barn, tacked-up horses in tow.

Uh-oh—if that was the regular Friday-afternoon inter-mediate adult lesson, that meant it was getting pretty late. And it was Maddie's turn to help make dinner. Normally it wouldn't be a big deal if she was a few minutes late, but her parents had only just forgotten about the Pink Twinkle incident. Maddie didn't want to give them any reason to get annoyed with her again so close to her birthday.

"Okay," she told Bridget. "Maybe you can ride longer next time."

After dinner, Maddie went upstairs to check in with the Pony Post. Tillie was out on a date, so she had the bed-room to herself.

There were several new postings from the others, along with a few photos. Maddie looked at the photos first. Nina had taken several artsy ones of Breezy grazing under a tree with drooping bunches of Spanish moss hanging down from its branches. Haley had posted a cute picture of Wings touching noses with a rangy brown-and-white dog.

Still smiling at that, Maddie scrolled down and scanned the postings.

[NINA] TGIF, everyone! Tough week in school; looking forward to a relaxing w/e!! I should finally have time to think of ways to keep Maddie in the good old US of A.

[HALEY] She doesn't only need to stay in the USA, tho. She needs to stay in CA, near Cloudy!!!

[NINA] LOL, I know. So, Mads, anything new to report?

[HALEY] I don't think she's checked in since last night. Maybe soon?

[BROOKE] Hi, all! Anyone still on?

[BROOKE] Oh well, guess not. Too bad, I need to vent to someone about my little sis and bro. They are STILL all into riding all of a sudden! Mom says it's just a phase and I should be patient. But it's hard to be

patient when I just want to ride my pony!!!

"I know how you feel," Maddie murmured. "Trust me!"

She glanced at the time stamp on Brooke's last message, wondering if she might still be on the site. But it had posted more than an hour earlier. Still, Maddie opened a new text box.

[MADDIE] Hi, guys! Brooke, I totally feel u re:

the kiddos. B/c I have barely been on Cloudy

all week! My friend Bridget is still into riding too.

Tho I'm hoping in her case it ISN'T a phase . . .

She went on to describe her plan to groom her friend to take over with Cloudy. Then she posted the message and sat back, scanning what she'd just written. When they read it, would the other Pony Posters think she was giving up too soon on staying in California? She opened another text box.

[MADDIE] Btw, I'm planning to talk to M&D after my

b'day to see if there's any chance this might not

happen. But I'm not holding my breath, so I need to start dealing with it, u know? I'll also need to talk to Bridget then. B/c so far she's not rly getting with the program. She seemed more interested in talking to the "cute" (according to her—and Vic, too) stall cleaner dude than in learning how to help get C ready. I'm just glad she didn't say anything embarrassing—for some reason she's convinced I have a crush on him, which is so not true. But that doesn't stop her from teasing me every chance she gets. . . . Anyway, when she finally got on Cloudy, she only walked around the ring about twice and then was ready to quit! Can u believe that?!? I mean, Ms. E practically has to drag me out of the saddle after a lesson's over, lol!

By the time Maddie posted the message, she was smiling. Somehow, just pouring out her problems to her Pony Post friends was making her feel better. After one last glance at her friends' photos, she logged off.

◆ CHAPTER ◆
9

MADDIE WOKE UP ON SATURDAY MORN-
ing feeling as if her brain were stuffed with cobwebs. She'd
fallen asleep a little later than usual, only to be awakened
when Tillie came crashing in from her date, making no
effort to be quiet. After that she'd lain awake in the dark
for a long time, trying to imagine what life in England
would be like. When she'd finally fallen back to sleep,
she'd been haunted by troubled dreams—some of them
involving Cloudy swimming across the English Channel.

With a yawn, she sat up. Glancing at the alarm
clock, she gritted her teeth when she saw that someone
had turned it off. Great. Now she was going to have to

hurry to be ready in time for her riding lesson.

"Thanks a lot, Tillie," she muttered, glaring at her sister's empty—and already neatly made—bed. It was tempting to go over and muss the sheets, since that was guaranteed to drive her tidy sister crazy. But Maddie resisted. She didn't need Tillie even more annoyed with her. Not with her party only a day away.

She rushed through a quick shower and an even quicker breakfast. Then she biked over to Solano Stables, arriving less than twenty minutes before her group lesson was scheduled to begin.

Dropping her bike outside the front entrance, she hurried inside. The grooming area was on the way to Cloudy's stall, and Maddie was startled to see the Chincoteague pony standing in the crossties. Bridget was fussing with Cloudy's forelock.

"Hey," Bridget said when she noticed Maddie. "I was starting to wonder if you were coming today."

"Overslept," Maddie replied. "Um, but I didn't know *you* were coming today."

Bridget shrugged. "It's such a nice day, I decided I was

in the mood for a ride. So I called Ms. Emerson this morning, and she said I could join your lesson again if I wanted."

"Oh." Maddie blinked, taking this in. "And she told you to ride Cloudy?"

"Not exactly." Bridget shot Maddie a sidelong look. "At first she was going to put me on some pony I never heard of, but that made me nervous. So I told her you offered to let me ride Cloudy again today."

"Oh yeah?" Maddie tried to tamp down her annoyance, but it bubbled up before she could stop it. "Well, if I'm giving up *another* ride on *my* pony, I hope at least you're planning to stay on for more than thirty seconds this time."

"What?" Bridget looked startled. Then she frowned. "Well, pardon me for not spending the entire day riding. I didn't realize there was a time limit. Or, you know, the opposite of that. Whatever."

She sounded flustered, the way she always did when she got upset. "Okay, whatever," Maddie muttered. "Sorry. I was just surprised, okay?"

Bridget put her hands on her hips. "If you don't want me to ride in your lesson, just say so!"

"Hey," Vic said as she and Val walked up just then, leading their assigned lesson ponies. "Um, is everything okay?"

"Sure." Maddie took a deep breath and forced a smile. "Everything's fine."

"Good." Val looked anxious as she glanced from Maddie to Bridget and back again. "Listen, Ms. Emerson wants us to pick out our ponies' stalls after the lesson if we have time."

"Okay," Maddie said.

"You mean pick up their poop?" Bridget wrinkled her nose. "Why?"

Vic shrugged. "Seth won't be here today, and she didn't have time to find someone else yet."

"Really?" Bridget's frown was back. "Well, Maddie will be the one who picks up Cloudy's poop. Because she obviously cares more about riding her favorite pony than being a good friend, so I might as well just leave."

"What?" Maddie wasn't sure whether to feel astonished, annoyed, or guilty, so she settled on all three. "No. Bridge, wait . . ."

It was too late. Bridget was already flouncing off down the aisle.

"What was that all about?" Vic asked, wide-eyed.

"I don't know." Maddie bit her lip. "Be right back."

She dashed after her friend. But by the time she reached the entrance, Bridget was nowhere in sight. Shoulders slumping, Maddie headed back inside.

While she was gone, the twins had clipped their ponies into the crossties on either side of Cloudy. Val looked up from picking her pony's hooves when Maddie reappeared.

"Where'd she go?" she asked.

Maddie sighed. "I guess she left."

"But I thought—" Vic began.

"Can we not talk about it right now, please?" Maddie cut her off. Guilt was already taking over from the other emotions. Maddie knew that Bridget was hurting these days and that she could be sensitive pretty much all the time. How could she have been so mean? Bridget had no way of knowing why it was so important to Maddie to spend time with Cloudy right now. How could she? Maddie hadn't told her.

"O-o-okay." Vic traded a look with her sister, then cleared her throat. "Anyway, we were just talking about Seth. Did you hear?"

"Hear what?" Maddie was barely paying attention as she picked up a brush and started working on Cloudy's coat.

"He quit," Vic said. "He won't be working here anymore."

That actually got Maddie's attention. "Really? Why?"

"I guess it was always supposed to be a temporary job," Val replied. "At least that's what Ms. E just told us. He was trying to earn enough quick money to buy his girlfriend a nice birthday gift."

Vic nodded. "She must have almost the same birthday as you, Mads."

"Yeah, guess so." Maddie was already losing interest. Sure, this meant Bridget wouldn't be able to embarrass her from now on by talking her up to Seth. But was that even an issue anymore? What if Bridget never wanted to ride again? That would be the end of Maddie's plan to turn her into Cloudy's new person.

Then another thought occurred to her. What if Bridget didn't get over their fight before Maddie's party tomorrow? She couldn't imagine celebrating what could be her last birthday in California without one of her very best friends.

Oh well, she thought, trying not to stress about it as she went to work on a manure stain on Cloudy's side. *I'll have to deal with that later. At least I get to ride my favorite pony today after all. . . .*

Maddie was feeling out of sorts when she arrived home a couple of hours later. She'd barely been able to enjoy riding Cloudy in the lesson, considering what had happened. Ms. Emerson had seemed surprised and a little annoyed by Bridget's sudden departure, which made Maddie feel worse than ever.

After the lesson, she'd been tempted to ride her bike over to Bridget's house and apologize. But she hadn't quite dared. For one thing, she probably needed to give her a little more time to cool off. For another thing, Maddie still wasn't quite ready to tell her about the move.

Maybe after my party, she thought as she dropped her bike in the garage. *If she still wants to come, that is . . .*

When she walked into the kitchen, her brothers were at the table munching on peanut butter and banana sandwiches. "Where's Mom?" Maddie asked them.

"Grocery store," Tyler said. "Dad didn't have time to go before he left for work."

Ryan nodded. "Tillie's watching us."

"Yeah." Tyler rolled his eyes. "But she made us make our own lunch."

"I can tell." Maddie glanced at the counter, which was smeared with stray blobs of peanut butter. A sticky knife was congealing to the edge of the sink, and a banana peel hung over the edge of the wastebasket.

Just then Tillie rushed into the room. "You're finally back," she said accusingly. "You need to watch the boys while I go out." She glanced around, wrinkling her nose in distaste. "And clean up this mess while you're at it."

"Whatever." Maddie wandered to the refrigerator to grab something to eat.

By the time she finished her lunch, Tillie was long gone and the boys were in the den playing video games. Maddie dumped her dishes in the sink.

"Ugh," she muttered, surveying the mess her brothers had left. "I guess I'd better get this cleaned up before Mom gets home."

She was tempted to drag the boys back in to do it. After all, it was their mess. And why should Maddie have to clean up after them—especially the day before her birthday?

Still, she knew it would be quicker and easier just to do it herself, so she did. Scrubbing icky, crusty peanut butter off the counter actually made her feel a tiny bit better—as if she were scrubbing away all the icky stuff that had happened that morning.

Finally the kitchen was sparkling clean, or at least close enough for Maddie's taste. She wiped her hands on a dishrag and headed for the stairs.

A few minutes later she was logged into the Pony Post. She'd been in such a rush that morning that it was her first chance today to check in, and she wanted to see if her friends had responded to last night's posting.

They had.

[BROOKE] Hi, Maddie. Sorry you didn't get to ride Cloudy again. As you know, I know how you feel! But I'm determined to ride my own pony today if it's the last thing I do, lol.

Just hoping the rain holds off. At least it's not
cold enough to snow here yet! Did you get
the snowstorm you were expecting, Haley?

[HALEY] Hi, B! Nope, no snow—it was a false
alarm. Which is awesome, since it means
Wings and I can have a nice, long schooling
session out on my cross-country field. We've
been working on a more balanced approach
to combination jumps lately, which is tricky,
since Wings and I both just want to ride
fast and leap over everything, lol! But we're
starting to get it. Hoping to do a little more
schooling before the snow comes for real
and the ground gets too hard & frozen for
jumping . . . But enough about me! Maddie, it
sounds like u are having a hard time w/ Bridget.
I still think u should just tell her what's going
on. Then she will understand, right? Just my
two cents, lol! Hope you have a good lesson
on Cloudy today. Let us know how it goes!

[NINA] Mads! Oh no, can't believe Bridget bogarted yr pony AGAIN!! H is right. U have to tell her!! But u can also tell her that the PP is going to figure out a way to keep u with Cloudy where u belong!!! Will check in later—off to the barn now myself. Happy riding this weekend, everyone!

[HALEY] Me again—just came back in from the barn. Brrr! It's getting cold out there. . . . Anyway, Maddie, I was thinking about you while I was getting Wings ready. And I remembered what you wrote about the way Bridget acted at the barn yesterday. I think I MIGHT have an idea about what's going on w/ her. . . . It's just a thought, but it might help u understand her pov. . . . Anyway, no time to type it out right now. My aunt is calling me—we're going into town to start some early holiday shopping. She loves having everything done early so she can sit back and enjoy the actual holidays, lol. Will write more later . . .

Maddie blinked, reading over Haley's last post again. Checking the time stamp, she saw that it had been posted about twenty minutes earlier, so Maddie had just missed her.

I wish she'd just typed out what she'd been thinking about Bridget, even if it was a quickie version. Maddie thought with a flash of curiosity. *She probably would've had time if she'd skipped the stuff about her aunt's shopping habits!*

She couldn't imagine what Haley could have come up with to explain Bridget's behavior. Scrolling back up to her own posting from the night before, she read through it and shook her head, still mystified.

Oh well. She would just have to wait until Haley signed on again. In the meantime, she opened a new text box.

[MADDIE] Sorry so late checking in! I slept late and had to book it to get to the barn in time. And guess what? When I got there, Bridget was already tacking up Cloudy to ride her in our lesson!!! I didn't even know she was thinking about coming today. And I guess maybe I was a little obvious about wanting to ride C myself, b/c Bridget got mad and ended up rushing off w/o riding at all. Oops. I feel really bad; need to make up w/ her before the party tomorrow . . . Gah! Why is my life so complicated right now? If this is what being 12 is going to be like, maybe I should stick with 11! LOL! Srsly tho, wish me luck. . . . And, Haley, I'm dying to hear yr theory about Bridget, whatever it is! Don't keep me in suspense!!

She signed off, then grabbed her cell phone and sent Bridget a text:

Sorry about this morning! Pls forgive me? You're still coming to my party tomorrow, right? B/c it wouldn't be the same without you. Text me back and tell me we're OK!!!

• CHAPTER •
10

"TURN OFF THE LIGHT ALREADY," TILLIE grumbled from her bed.

Maddie ignored her, scrolling up and down through the last few postings on the Pony Post, hoping she'd somehow missed Haley's. But no—there was nothing new from her since the post Maddie had seen after lunch.

Glancing at the alarm clock, Maddie sighed. It was almost ten thirty p.m. Pacific time, which meant Haley was surely sound asleep by now. Why hadn't she posted again?

Oh well. As she logged off, Maddie told herself that Haley probably had a good reason for not being able to post yet. She just had to be patient, and she would hear from Haley sooner or later.

She wasn't so sure about Bridget. Maddie had been checking her phone all day, but Bridget had never responded to her text. Setting her laptop aside, Maddie grabbed the phone off her bedside table and checked again. Still nothing.

"Light?" Tillie's tone was icy.

"Okay, okay." Maddie set the phone down, then reached over and switched off the lamp on her bedside table. Whatever Bridget's problem was, Maddie would have to deal with it in the morning.

When Maddie opened her eyes on Sunday morning, the room was bright and filled with sun. She glanced over at Tillie's bed, but it was empty.

"So this is what being twelve feels like," Maddie said aloud as she sat up and stretched.

Reaching for her phone, she found a few texts from friends wishing her a happy birthday. Most of them also mentioned that they were looking forward to the party later. But there was still nothing from Bridget.

Maddie bit her lip, wondering what to do. Noticing her laptop lying where she'd set it the night before, she grabbed it and logged on to the Pony Post. All three of her friends had already checked in to say happy birthday; Nina had even included a GIF of a dancing horse that looked almost like Cloudy, which made Maddie smile.

Then she spotted Haley's second posting:

[HALEY] Btw, sorry I never got back here last night. Hope u weren't in too much suspense, Maddie! We ended up running into some friends of the family in town and went back to their place for dinner, then had to rush to do chores before it got too dark and cold. By the time that was finished, all I could think about was falling into bed, lol!

Maddie nodded as she read. Haley's life seemed so different from hers sometimes! It was easy to forget that not everyone was the same, living in a regular suburban house, playing soccer after school, and visiting her pony at the boarding barn. That was Maddie's life, but it wasn't anything like Haley's, who lived on her family's farm and did all the daily care for Wings herself. Her chores weren't anything like Maddie's, either—instead of loading the dishwasher and vacuuming the living room, Haley had to help feed animals, load hay into the loft, and who knew what other farm-type activities. And most of it happened every day, all year round, even in the frosty, snowy Wisconsin winters.

I wonder if my new life in London will seem as foreign to me as Haley's life does now, Maddie thought.

But she quickly shrugged that off, continuing to read.

[HALEY] Anyway, here's my theory about Bridget. I don't know her, of course, so I could be totally off base. But when you wrote that stuff about her teasing you about the cute boy, it reminded me of my friends Tracey and Emma. Remember? I've told you guys about them— they suddenly went boy crazy last summer and practically turned into different people. At least, it seems that way sometimes! Anyway, they're always acting the way Bridget is now about

the cute stall cleaner guy, teasing each other

& stuff. It made me wonder if maybe she has a

crush on him herself. That could be why she's

hanging around the barn so much lately even

tho she doesn't seem that interested in riding.

(Actually, it kinda sounds like she might be a little

bit afraid of horses??) And that could be why

she's teasing you about him. She doesn't want

to admit SHE is the one w/ the crush! I know

that doesn't make much sense, lol, but like I

said, I've seen it myself w/ my friends! Anyway,

just a theory, u know? But think about it. . . .

This time Maddie was shaking her head as she finished reading. Haley was way off base. Bridget didn't have a crush on Seth—she thought *Maddie* did. Right?

She thought back over the past week. About how Bridget couldn't seem to stop teasing her about Seth—how cute he was, how he was such a good athlete, and all the rest.

But suddenly, that wasn't all she remembered about the way Bridget had been acting. She also remembered how her friend suddenly wanted to be at the barn all the time—ever since that first visit when she'd met Seth. Coincidence? Maybe not. There was also the way Bridget had started noticing and talking about pony poop much more than Maddie might have expected. And also how she'd ignored most of Maddie's grooming and tacking lesson to chitchat with Seth about football.

"Oh wow," Maddie said aloud as everything suddenly started to make sense. Could Haley be right? Was Bridget really hiding her own interest in Seth by acting like she thought Maddie was crushing on him? Come to think of it, that did sort of sound like something she might do. . . .

Then there was yesterday. Yeah, Maddie had started their fight with her snide comment. But normally something like that wouldn't be enough to send Bridget rushing off in a snit. That hadn't happened until they'd heard from Vic and Val that Seth wouldn't be coming to the barn that day.

"Bingo," Maddie murmured with a half smile. How had she missed it before?

♦ ♦ ♦

When Maddie coasted down the driveway to Solano Stables a short while later, Vic and Val were waiting for her outside the main doors.

"Happy birthday!" they sang out in unison as Maddie leaned her bike against the wall.

"Thanks." Maddie smiled and hugged them both, then peered past them into the barn. "Is Bridget here?"

"Haven't seen her," Val said.

Vic shoved a small wrapped gift at Maddie. "Here," she said. "You need to open this now."

"Are you sure?" Maddie turned the package over in her hands. "Shouldn't I wait until the party?"

"No, now," Vic said with a grin. "You'll see why."

Maddie wasn't going to argue any further. She loved opening gifts!

She ripped the tidy bow off first, guessing that Val had tied it—Vic could barely tie the laces of her paddock boots without ending up with tangles. Next came the pretty floral paper. Inside was a small, brightly colored bottle. As she looked at it, Maddie was confused for a second—but then she laughed as she realized what it was.

"Pink Twinkle!" she exclaimed.

Vic grinned. "Not quite—we weren't about to spend that much on nail polish. Not even for your birthday."

"But it was the closest we could find to the same color," Val said. "We figured we could touch up Cloudy's hooves before the party."

"It's perfect! Thank you." Maddie hugged each of them again. Most of the nail polish had worn off the pony's hooves by then, though there were still a few streaks of sparkly pink. Now she would look party perfect! "But don't tell Tillie, okay?" Maddie added with a grin.

Vic and Val laughed. "Promise!" Val said.

"Now, come on." Vic grabbed Maddie's hand. "Let's go put it on her so it has time to dry."

Maddie allowed them to drag her off to Cloudy's stall, though she couldn't help glancing at the entrance over her shoulder. Bridget had been planning to be here by now to help with the party setup. But that was before . . . Was she still going to show?

An hour later, Cloudy had been groomed within an

inch of her life and all four hooves painted with sparkly pink polish. Val was braiding matching pink ribbons into her mane when Bridget finally appeared.

"Hi," she said, not quite meeting Maddie's eye. "Sorry about yesterday."

"Me too." Maddie could tell that Bridget felt awkward. Well, she'd had enough of that—it was time to get things back to normal. So she stepped forward and grabbed her in a big hug. For a second Bridget felt tense, but then she relaxed and hugged Maddie back.

"Happy birthday," she said into her hair.

"Thanks." Maddie pulled away. "I wasn't sure if you'd come."

Bridget shrugged, still keeping her eyes down. "How could I miss such a momentous occasion?"

Maddie wondered which play she'd picked up that phrase from, though she didn't bother to ask. "It's just too bad my boyfriend won't be here, huh?" she said lightly.

"What?" Bridget blinked at her. "Oh, you mean Seth?"

"Yeah." Maddie ignored the twins, who were trading a slightly perplexed glance behind Bridget's back. "We found out he's not going to be working here anymore. He was just trying to earn money to buy his girlfriend something nice."

"His girlfriend?" Bridget frowned for a second as she processed that. "Oh. Too bad for you, huh?"

"Yeah, too bad." Maddie was tempted to call her on it, make her admit what had really been going on with the whole Seth thing. But maybe it was better to leave it be. Bridget could be funny about things sometimes—sort of like Brooke, who wasn't always as blunt as the other three Pony Posters. That meant Maddie and the others had to be tactful to get her to open up when something was bugging her. Bridget wasn't shy like Brooke could be, but she also required a little extra finesse to convince her to talk about certain things.

But why bother in this case? Tillie and her friends were always joking around about rebound guys—the ones they went out with for a little while after getting dumped by the ones they really liked. Maybe Seth had been sort of the same thing for Bridget.

Maddie shook her head slightly, getting another twinge of the funny feeling she'd had while thinking about Haley's life earlier. As if she were looking at someone from a foreign country, one where she didn't speak the language very well.

At least I won't have to worry about that in London, she thought, her mind jumping from one problem to another.

Meanwhile Bridget stepped over and gave Cloudy a pat. "Oh well. Seth didn't do a very good job of keeping your poop picked up anyway, did he, Cloudy?"

"Yeah," Maddie said, banishing all thoughts of England. "Hey, we have plenty of time before the party's supposed to start. Want to take a pony ride on Cloudy? It's the least we could do since you didn't get to ride yesterday."

"Oh." Bridget moved away from the pony. "Um, that's okay. Actually, I'm thinking maybe riding isn't for me, you know?"

"Really?" Vic said. "Are you sure?"

Bridget shrugged. "It was fun to learn the basics, though," she said with a smile. "Now I'll be ready if I ever have an acting job where I have to ride a horse, right?"

Vic and Val laughed, but Maddie's heart sank. So much for her plan to turn Bridget and Cloudy into the perfect new pair. . . .

She shook off her disappointment as quickly as it came. At least hanging out at the barn had helped Bridget forget her heartbreak. That was the important thing, right? Maddie would just have to get her Cloudy news from Vic and Val and her other friends at the barn.

"Guess we should start setting up for the party," she said. "Ms. Emerson said she'd make sure the tractor and stuff were out of the way by the time I got here, but I should go check."

"We'll do it," Val volunteered, nudging her sister.

"Yeah," Vic agreed. "You stay here and hang with Cloudy."

"Okay, thanks." As the twins hurried off, Maddie shot Bridget a sidelong glance.

Bridget looked over just in time to catch her eye. "What?" she demanded. "You're not still mad at me, are you?"

Maddie stepped over to rub Cloudy's face. "I was never mad at you," she said. "I was just being selfish about Cloudy and took it out on you." She hesitated, not sure whether to continue. "Um . . ."

Bridget narrowed her eyes. "What? There's something you're not telling me. Spill it, Martinez. All my acting training makes me excellent at reading human expressions, so you can't hide from me."

Maddie kept her gaze on Cloudy's big, liquid brown eyes, not sure what to do. She hadn't been planning to say anything about the move until after the party. But was that the best way to be a good friend? She'd never kept something so important from Bridget before. Or from Vic and Val, for that matter. Maddie's life was usually an open book, and it felt weird to have secrets.

Cloudy shifted her weight, turning her head to snuffle at Maddie's arm. Maddie fished a treat out of her pocket and let the pony lip it off her palm. Suddenly the whole idea of leaving Cloudy behind—of leaving everyone and everything behind again, just when her life was going so great—was almost overwhelming.

"Okay, I wasn't going to tell you this until after the party, but I can't stand it anymore," she blurted out, turning to face Bridget. "See, I found out something kind of crazy the other day. . . ."

The rest of the story tumbled out of her. As she listened, Bridget's eyes got wider and wider.

"Noooo!" she wailed when Maddie finished. "This is some kind of weird birthday prank or something, right? Because you can't move away! Especially not to a whole new country! I mean, who does that?"

Maddie sighed. "I wish it was a prank. But it's not."

Bridget grabbed her by the shoulders, sort of hugging her and shaking her at the same time. "Seriously, Mads. Is this for real? Your mom got transferred to *England*?"

"Looks that way."

Suddenly Bridget pushed her away so forcefully that Maddie stumbled backward and had to catch herself on Cloudy's warm, solid side. Bridget didn't seem to notice; she was glaring in the direction of the stable entrance.

"Your parents will be here soon for the party, right?" she said. "Let me talk to them—I'll make them see that this is a huge mistake."

"No!" Maddie's heart thumped in alarm. "Listen to me, Bridge. You can't say anything to anyone right now, okay? I don't want to ruin my birthday."

"Too late." Bridget stuck out her lower lip in a pout.

"I mean it," Maddie warned. "Nobody knows. Well, obviously my parents do, I guess. But they don't know that I know. And Tillie and the boys have no clue. I haven't breathed a word to anyone except the Pony Post."

"The what?" Bridget blinked. "Oh, the website thing. You mean you told them before you told me?"

"Sorry." Maddie shrugged. "You were so depressed about the Tony thing already. I just figured . . ."

"Yeah, okay, I get it." Bridget sighed, gazing at her with troubled brown eyes. "This is horrible, Mads."

"I know." Maddie reached over and squeezed her shoulder. "We can talk about it more after the party. Okay?"

Bridget nodded. "Don't worry. I won't say anything."

"Good. But you can't walk around looking like someone died, either, okay?" Maddie said. "Nobody's going to believe you're that worked up about dumb old Tony."

The ghost of a smile flitted across Bridget's face. Then she straightened her shoulders. "Don't worry. I'm an actress, remember?" She pasted on a huge grin. "Your secret is safe with me."

◆ CHAPTER ◆
11

MADDIE AND BRIDGET WERE SILENT FOR a few minutes after that, each of them lost in her own thoughts as they brushed Cloudy's glossy palomino coat. Then Maddie heard the chatter of the twins coming down the aisle.

"Remember, they don't know," she whispered to Bridget.

Bridget nodded, then pantomimed zipping her lips. "Hey, guys." She greeted Vic and Val in a cheerful voice. "Took you long enough. Did you have to drag that tractor out yourself, or what?"

Vic giggled. "Nope, everything's out of the way. We just stopped to say hi to some of the ponies."

"Cool." Bridget dropped the brush she was using back into the grooming bucket. "So that means it's time to put up the decorations, right?"

"We'd better hurry." Maddie checked her watch. "Mom and Dad will be here with the food in like an hour and a half, and everyone else should start getting here pretty soon after that."

"Eh, eh, eh!" Bridget waggled a finger in her face. "What's this 'we' business? You can't set up for your own party. The three of us will take care of it. Right, girls?"

"Sure," Val said, and Vic nodded and shot Maddie a thumbs-up.

Maddie barely saw it. She was gazing at Bridget, feeling kind of impressed. If she hadn't known better, she'd never have guessed that her friend had a care in the world right now beyond streamers and balloons.

What do you know? she thought. *I guess she really is a good actress—even when she has to make up her own lines.*

"Okay. That's nice of you guys to offer," she told all three of her friends. "But what do you expect me to do while you're working—sit here and twiddle my thumbs?"

"Duh." Vic gestured toward the pony standing behind Maddie. "You've got just enough time for a nice, relaxing birthday ride on Cloudy."

"Don't worry," Val added. "Ms. Emerson already said it was okay. Just don't leave the regular trails."

"Really?" Maddie couldn't help a little flash of happiness. Finally she would have her favorite pony all to herself for a while—guilt free. "Okay. In that case, thanks, you guys!"

A few minutes later she was riding out past the ring, heading for the public multi-use trails that wound through the local fields, forests, and vineyard-dotted foothills. Cloudy's ears were pricked, and she felt eager to go.

"You love exploring, don't you, girl?" Maddie leaned forward and patted Cloudy on the neck. "Maybe it reminds you of being on Assateague Island when you were a foal."

She smiled at the image of baby Cloudy trotting and cantering around the sandy dunes of Assateague, stopping only long enough to nibble on the salty cordgrass growing in the local marshes before galloping off through the surf. Thanks to reading and rereading *Misty of Chincoteague* and its sequels, Maddie could picture it perfectly, even though she'd never been there.

Then the images faded and she glanced around at the familiar trails she'd ridden on so often over the past couple of years. How many more times would she get to see them?

Probably not many, she thought, stopping herself from adding up the days. *So I'd better make sure to enjoy it while I can.*

"Don't worry, Cloudy," she said as the mare ambled along the sun-dappled path beneath a line of tall valley oaks that separated the trail from a road. "I'll come back and visit you. I promise. As often as I can."

She bit her lip, once again trying not to think too much about the details. England was a long way away, and plane tickets were expensive—that was what her parents were always saying whenever the kids pestered them to visit their relatives in other states or take vacations in various far-flung spots. Tyler wanted to see New York City, Ryan was dying to go to Cape Canaveral in Florida, and Tillie had been agitating for a trip to Paris for as long as Maddie could remember.

Maybe she'll finally get to go there, she thought. *Paris is a lot closer to London than to California.*

Cloudy stepped out into a sunny clearing, and Maddie squinted, glad that the weather was so nice—bright, a little breezy, low sixties. Not bad for November, especially compared to the stuff Haley had been writing lately about the snow and cold in Wisconsin. Maddie was pretty sure it didn't snow much in England, though she'd heard it was kind of rainy and gloomy a lot of the time.

"Forget about that," she told herself out loud. "It's time to live in the moment."

That was a phrase she'd heard a lot from her dad and various other people. Maddie had never thought about it much before, and now she realized why. Normally she had no trouble living in the moment. Why do anything else?

But now it was much harder, knowing that this moment was part of a countdown to something very different. And for once she couldn't just look forward to the adventure. She had to deal with the sadness of leaving something very important behind, knowing that things would never be the same.

"But I don't have to deal with it right this second, do I?" she murmured, nudging the pony into a trot. "Right now I just want to enjoy this moment."

And for the rest of the ride, she did her very best to do just that.

"Thanks for inviting me, Maddie." Coach Wu, Maddie's soccer coach, came toward Maddie, clutching a cup of punch in one hand and a cookie in the other. "This is fun. Now I understand why you always rush off to this place right after practice."

"I'm glad you could come." Maddie smiled at the coach, though it felt a little forced.

Her party had been in full swing for more than an hour. By the time Maddie had returned from her trail ride, her friends had the barn decorated to the hilt. Soon after that, Maddie's family had arrived, bearing boxes and coolers full of food and drink. Ms. Emerson had helped them set up three large folding tables along the wall. Sergeant Martinez's best punch bowl went on one, with Ryan and Tyler proudly pouring in the bright purple concoction they'd helped mix at home. Another table was laid out with platters of cookies, chips and dips, her father's spicy homemade empanadas, and various other finger foods, while the third table was intended to hold gifts.

By the time everything was ready, Maddie's friends had started to arrive. Vic switched on the music, Bridget started to dance, and the party was on. Everyone seemed to be having a good time—even Tillie was smiling as she led her boyfriend around by the hand.

Maddie was trying to have fun—to live in the moment—but she wasn't quite feeling it. How could she enjoy herself when she knew she'd probably never see most of these people again after January?

Snap out of it, girl, she chided herself as Coach Wu wandered off to talk to some of Maddie's teammates. *Someone's going to notice you're acting all emo.*

She pasted on a bright smile as she heard footsteps behind her. When she turned and saw that it was Bridget, she relaxed.

"Oh, it's you," she said.

"Are you okay?" Bridget peered at her. "Because I'm

totally not. This is all such a huge farce! How can your parents act so carefree when they know they're about to rip you away from everything good and wonderful in your life?"

Okay, that was a little dramatic even for Bridget. "Chill," Maddie told her, glancing around to make sure nobody was close enough to hear them. "We just have to deal with it, okay? At least until the party's over."

"Whatever," Bridget muttered, looking sulky. "I'm just saying."

At that moment Maddie's father whistled for attention. "Thanks for coming, everyone," he said. "I think it's time to get to Maddie's favorite part of the day."

"Presents!" Tyler shouted.

Everyone laughed and applauded. "Yes, come open your gifts, Maddie," her mother said. "Is there a chair?"

Ms. Emerson appeared, pushing her wheeled office chair toward the gift table. "Here you go, Maddie." She patted the seat. "Make yourself comfortable."

"Thanks." Maddie made her way forward. "Thanks, everyone."

She took her seat and looked around at her party guests. Vic and Val were smiling at her from the front of the crowd. Nearby, a couple of her soccer teammates were petting one of the barn cats. Several school friends were hanging out near the refreshments, and Coach Wu was chatting with one of Maddie's neighbors over by the punch bowl.

Everyone Maddie cared about from this place was here, and for a second she felt as if she might start crying. How could she leave all this behind?

"Maddie." Her mother leaned closer. "Are you okay? You look odd."

"I'm fine." Maddie tried to channel Bridget's acting skills as she grinned at her mother. "Uh, it's just kind of weird being so old, you know?"

Her mother laughed. "Did you hear that?" she joked to Ms. Emerson with a wink. "Talk about making someone feel old . . ."

"Here, open this one first." Vic darted forward and tossed a large but lightweight wrapped gift into Maddie's lap. "It's from us."

"Okay." Maddie ripped into the package and held up a blue saddle pad. "Cool! I love it."

"We thought that color would look nice on Cloudy," Val called out. "But you can exchange it for a different color if you want."

"No she can't," Vic said. "That color's perfect!"

Everyone laughed, including Maddie, though she couldn't help feeling a little sad. The blue pad *would* look nice against Cloudy's pale palomino spots. Too bad Maddie would probably get to see it on her only a few times before she moved.

"Open mine next!" One of Maddie's school friends pushed forward and handed over another package.

Maddie set the saddle pad aside to unwrap the new gift. She *ooh*ed and *aah*ed over the book the girl had given her, then moved on to the next package.

As she unwrapped gift after gift, Maddie did her best to be grateful. Everyone had gone out of their way to get her things she'd like, and she really did appreciate that. How could they know that the only gift she really wanted was to be able to stay here with Cloudy and all her friends?

By the time she neared the end of the pile of gifts, her face was starting to hurt from smiling so hard. Then Tyler grabbed one of the last wrapped packages.

"This one's from all of us," he said, dropping it in Maddie's lap. "Me and Ry and Tillie, I mean."

"It was mostly Tillie's idea," Ryan spoke up.

Maddie glanced at her sister, who was leaning against her boyfriend over by the stalls. Tillie smiled and waggled her fingers at Maddie. Did that mean she'd finally gotten over the nail polish thing? Maddie hoped so. For one thing, she didn't relish the thought of a long plane ride to London with Tillie mad at her in the next seat. . . .

"What are you waiting for?" Tyler broke into her thoughts, sounding impatient. "Open it already!"

Maddie laughed. "Okay, okay." She ripped off the paper to reveal a flat cardboard box. When she opened it, she gasped. Inside, nestled in tissue paper, was a beautiful tortoiseshell frame—with a photo of her and Cloudy.

"Tillie took the picture," Tyler explained, darting forward to peer at it. "We thought we should use one of you guys jumping or doing something more exciting, but she thought this one was better."

"It's beautiful." Maddie couldn't stop staring at the photograph. It had captured a quiet moment between her and Cloudy. The mare had her ears pricked and an alert look in her kind eyes. Maddie was holding her lead rope, gazing at the pony with a soft smile. Maddie had no idea when Tillie had taken it, but it was perfect.

Bridget stepped forward to look at it over her shoulder. "Oh, it's gorgeous!" she exclaimed. "It'll be a great memento you can take with you to remember Cloudy by."

"Yeah," Maddie said, then froze, realizing what Bridget had just said.

"To remember her by?" Tyler sounded confused. "What do you mean?"

"Is Cloudy going somewhere?" Ryan added.

"No, it's nothing," Maddie blurted out. "Uh, Bridget was just kidding around."

"It's a line from a play," Bridget said at the same time. She shot Maddie a guilty look. "Um, I mean I was kidding around."

Ms. Emerson raised an eyebrow. "You're not planning to stop riding Cloudy anytime soon, are you, Maddie?"

"No," Maddie said. "I mean, I don't want to. I mean . . ." She glanced at her parents, thinking it was about time for them to jump in. After all, they had to know that the cat was pretty much out of the bag. . . .

But both of them looked confused. "What's the matter, Maddie?" her father asked. "You look like you have indigestion or something."

"It's okay." Maddie stared at her father meaningfully, then shifted her gaze to her mother. "I know."

Her mother blinked at her. "Know what?"

Maddie sighed. Did they have to make this more difficult than it already was? She glanced at her little brothers, wishing they didn't have to hear the news this way—in front of a crowd, on what was supposed to be a happy occasion. But whatever. She couldn't help that.

"I know we're moving again," she said. "To London."

Gasps came from all around. "You're *moving*?" someone shrieked—Maddie thought it might have been Vic, though she didn't look over to check for sure. She was staring at her parents, who looked perplexed.

"Moving?" Maddie's father glanced at his wife, his lips twitching slightly. "Is there something you haven't shared with me, honey?"

Bridget gasped. "You didn't even tell your *husband*?" she exclaimed, staring at Sergeant Martinez.

"We're not moving—are we, Mom?" Ryan sounded worried.

Tillie was pushing forward, looking agitated. "Mom, Dad?" she exclaimed. "Tell me this isn't true!"

Maddie felt terrible. All three of her siblings looked totally freaked out. "I'm sorry," she told her mother. "I saw the plane confirmation thingy by accident. I swear I wasn't poking around in your office. I just went to plug in my laptop and—"

"Hold on!" Maddie's mother held up her hands, silencing everyone with her sternest military tone. Then she looked at Maddie. "This is about the plane tickets to London? The paper in my desk drawer?"

"Yes," Maddie said. "I didn't say anything before because I knew you'd be mad, but I know we're going to

London." She shot a look at her siblings. "In January."

Tillie's gasp echoed through the barn. "We're moving in *January*?"

Tyler's lower lip quivered. "Mom?"

Their mother held up a hand again. "Okay, this isn't how I'd planned to tell you all," she said. "But it's true. The whole family will be heading over to London in January."

· CHAPTER ·

12

MADDIE'S HEART BARELY HAD TIME TO sink when her mother spoke again. "Yes, we're going to London," Sergeant Martinez said, raising her voice above new gasps from everyone else. "But we're not *moving* there. Those tickets are for a family vacation."

"What?" Tillie shrieked. Then she raced back and flung herself into her boyfriend's arms. "Did you hear that, sweetie? I'm not leaving!"

Maddie just stared at her parents. They were trading a look—her father was smiling, and her mother was rolling her eyes and looking mildly exasperated.

"It's true, kids," Mr. Martinez said. "Your cousin Ronnie

had more frequent-flier miles than he could ever use, so we worked out a deal."

Maddie's mother nodded. "It was supposed to be a surprise Christmas gift."

"Oops." Maddie was so stunned she wasn't sure how to react for a second. "Um, sorry for ruining the surprise. But this is for real? We're not moving?"

"Not anytime soon," her father assured her. "In fact, your mother's been talking to her supervisors about taking on some new responsibilities at the base."

"That's right," his wife said. "Which means the Air Force isn't likely to be sending me anywhere for a while."

"This is amazing!" Bridget grabbed Maddie in a big bear hug. "You're not leaving! *And* you get to go to London, too!" She pulled away, pouting. "Which I'm super-jealous about, by the way."

"Yeah, I'll send you a postcard." Maddie shot a look around at her other friends. Vic and Val still looked a little confused—Maddie knew she'd have to apologize for not telling them sooner. But maybe it was just as well. She'd been worried for nothing, but at least nobody else except

Bridget had wasted any time worrying with her. And the Pony Post, of course.

Her father squeezed her shoulder. "Hope you weren't too freaked out, birthday girl," he said. "But I thought you knew better than to jump to conclusions."

"Guess not," Maddie admitted sheepishly. "But now that I'm twelve and so much more mature, I'm sure I'll do better from now on."

That made him chuckle. Maddie smiled, suddenly feeling much more in a party mood. She clapped her hands.

"Hey, who turned the music down?" she exclaimed. "I feel like dancing!"

A few hours later, the party was over and everyone had left except Maddie and her family. Ms. Emerson was off at the other end of the barn, beginning the evening feeding, and even Vic and Val had reluctantly headed home for dinner. While her parents and siblings packed up the leftover food and decorations, Maddie slipped away.

"Hey, baby girl," she murmured, letting herself into Cloudy's stall.

The mare had been snoozing in the corner, but she came forward to greet Maddie with a soft snuffle. Maddie smiled, wrapping her arms around the pony's warm, furry neck.

"Did you hear the news?" she whispered. "I'm not going anywhere."

Cloudy nuzzled her shirt, looking for a treat. Maddie laughed and hugged her again. Hearing her mother calling from somewhere down the aisle, she planted a kiss on the pony's nose.

"Gotta go," she said. "But don't worry. I'll be back."

Smiling at the thought of all the rides ahead of them, she left the stall and hurried to find her family. She arrived just in time to help finish loading stuff into the trunk.

"It's about time you came to help, considering this was all for you." Tillie's words were grumpy, but her voice and expression were mild as she handed Maddie a box of paper cups.

"Yeah, thanks again, everyone." Maddie stuck the box in the trunk and brushed off her hands. Then she turned to her sister. "By the way, Tillie, I really am sorry about the nail polish thing. I swear I didn't realize the stuff was that crazy expensive or I never would've borrowed it." Seeing her sister's expression turn a bit sour, she quickly added, "I mean swiped it. And it doesn't matter—I shouldn't have taken it even if it only cost ten cents. Sorry."

"Hmmph." Tillie shrugged. "Whatever. That color probably wouldn't look that good on me anyway, I guess." She glanced at her flawlessly manicured nails, which were painted a pale shade of lavender.

Maddie's father winked as he hurried past with the punch bowl. "Peace reigns again in the Martinez household," he said. "For how long, I wonder."

At that moment Ryan let out a squeal. "Hey!" Maddie's mother shouted from the doorway, where she'd just emerged with a shopping bag stuffed with some of Maddie's gifts. "Ty, stop pinching your brother!"

Maddie's father sighed and smiled. "Not long, it seems." He stowed the punch bowl in the trunk, then winked again at Maddie. "Which just means everything's back to normal, eh?"

"Definitely." Maddie grinned at him.

Soon they were packed into the car for the short drive home. Maddie's mother spent most of it chiding Maddie—and the rest of the kids—about snooping, keeping secrets, and various other transgressions. But Maddie could tell she wasn't as annoyed as she was trying to sound.

"Sorry, Mom," she said contritely when her mother paused for breath. "It won't happen again."

"Yeah, right." Tillie rolled her eyes. "But listen, about this trip—we're really going to London?"

"Absolutely." Mr. Martinez smiled at her in the rearview mirror. "Are you excited?"

"Totally!" Tillie's eyes shone. "I can't wait to see Harrods in person!"

"Who's Harry?" Ryan asked absently, glancing up from the comic book he'd started flipping through during his mother's speech.

"Duh!" Tyler poked him. "He's one of those English princes Tillie's always mooning over on TV."

Tillie frowned at them both. "Not Harry—*Harrods*,"

she said. "It's an extremely famous department store."

Maddie exchanged a shrug with her brothers. She'd never heard of Harrods either. But she was looking forward to seeing it—and everything else in London too!

"Hey, I saw that brochure about riding in London," she said. "Are we going to do that?"

Her parents traded a look. "With all that snooping, I can't believe you didn't find your gifts, Maddie," her mother said with a snort. "But yes, we're looking into the riding thing."

"I don't have to go, do I?" Tillie wrinkled her nose. "I'm not going all the way to England to do something I could do right here at home."

"Not that you ever come riding with me here, either," Maddie said, thinking briefly of Brooke and her complaints about her sister and brother wanting to ride Foxy.

Tillie shrugged. "So not the point."

Her father chuckled. "We'll have to work out a schedule as the trip gets closer," he said. "We'll only be there for a week, and we don't want to miss anything."

No, Maddie thought, glancing at the bag of gifts tucked

between her feet. The photo of her and Cloudy was peeking out the top. *We definitely don't want to miss anything.* She smiled and turned her head to watch the familiar scenery slide past the car window, letting the rest of her family's conversation wash over her.

When they got home, Maddie helped unpack the car and then headed upstairs. She wanted to let the Pony Post know her good news right away. When she logged in, there were several new messages.

[BROOKE] Happy birthday (again), Maddie! Let us know how the party went.

[HALEY] Ya, and don't worry about the other stuff. We'll figure something out.

[NINA] Or die trying, lol. (That's what my dad always says when he doesn't think someone can actually do something. But in this case, I KNOW we can!!!)

[NINA] Oh yeah, and happy b'day again
from me too! Hope you could forget
everything & enjoy the party!

Maddie smiled. After the good news about the London trip had come out, the rest of her party had been practically perfect. The only thing that could have made it better was if her Pony Post friends had been there. But she'd have to settle for sharing it with them now. Opening a text box, she started to type.

[MADDIE] I'm back! Thanx for the extra
b'day wishes! The party was super-fun.
About a zillion people came, and I think
everyone had a good time. But I'll tell u
more about that later. First I have some
AMAZING news: WE'RE NOT MOVING!!!!

She posted that much and then sat back, waiting to see if anyone responded. When no new messages popped up, she shrugged. She'd been hoping to catch one or more of her friends on the site live, but it seemed none of them were there.

Because I know if they were, they'd post back right away after news like that! she thought with a smile.

Then she opened another text box:

[MADDIE] Yeah, here's how it went down. I ended up telling Bridget everything before the party, and she was freaked out, of course. . . .

She typed fast, filling in the rest of the details. Her ride on Cloudy. How weird it was to try to act normal when she thought her whole world was about to change. The gorgeous photograph Tillie and the boys had given her. Bridget's thoughtless comment. And finally, her parents' news about those tickets to London.

[MADDIE] . . . Isn't that great? So I get to see London—but then I get to come home to Cloudy and the rest afterward. It's perfect!!!!!

She posted that too and sat back again, thinking over everything that had happened. Her father was right—she'd jumped to conclusions, and the result was days of pointless worry. Not to mention that fight with Bridget. If Maddie hadn't been so worried about leaving Cloudy behind forever, she never would have been so freaked out by missing a few rides.

That reminded her of something else she'd wanted to tell her Pony Post friends. She started typing again.

[MADDIE] Btw, Brooke, I hope your lil bro and sis are letting you ride Foxy again by now. B/c I def. know how you feel about having to share. I mean, I'm used to having to share Cloudy with other lesson students and stuff. But it was still rough being expected to share MY Cloudy with someone else all the time— even tho that someone else is one of my bffs!! I'm just glad Bridget forgave me and we're cool again. And, Haley, u were right about the boy thing. The stall cleaner quit, and now

Bridget doesn't even want to ride anymore.

Even tho I'm sorry she won't still be coming

to the barn with me (at least not very often),

I'm happy to have Cloudy all to myself again.

(Well, sort of . . . U know what I mean!) It's

like getting my favorite pony as an extra-

special birthday gift! Happy birthday to me!

◆ Glossary ◆

Chincoteague pony: A breed of pony found on Assateague Island, which lies off the coasts of Maryland and Virginia. Chincoteague ponies are sometimes referred to as wild horses, but are more properly called "feral" since they are not native to the island but were brought there by humans sometime many years past. There are several theories about how this might have happened, including the one told in the classic novel *Misty of Chincoteague* by Marguerite Henry. That novel also details the world-famous pony swim and auction that still take place in the town of Chincoteague to this day.

bay: A color of horse or pony. Bays have a reddish-brown coat with black mane, tail, and lower legs.

body brush: A grooming brush with soft bristles used on the body of a horse or pony.

chin strap: Part of the helmet; the chin strap snaps beneath the rider's chin and helps keep the helmet on the head.

grooming kit: A collection of brushes, currycombs, and other tools used to groom a horse or pony.

lead rope: A rope, usually with a clip on one end, used to lead a horse or pony. Lead ropes can be made of various materials, including cotton, nylon, or leather.

lesson horse/pony: A horse or pony ridden primarily in riding lessons. Lesson horses tend to be quiet, agreeable, and well trained, since they usually must carry a variety of riders rather than just one or two. However, some stables also keep livelier, more challenging lesson horses for more experienced lesson riders.

noseband: The noseband (sometimes called a "cavesson") is the part of the bridle that goes around the horse's nose on an English bridle. There are several kinds of nosebands, including flash, drop, or figure-eight nosebands. Standard Western bridles usually don't include a noseband.

rump: Also known as the "croup," a horse or pony's rump is the top of the horse's hindquarters and the area around it.

saddle pad: A pad that goes between the horse's back and the saddle. A saddle pad keeps the underside of the saddle clean and can sometimes be used to help a saddle fit better.

throatlatch: A strap on a bridle or halter that goes beneath the horse's throat. It prevents the bridle from coming off over the horse's head.

Marguerite Henry's Ponies of Chincoteague is inspired by the award-winning books by Marguerite Henry, the beloved author of such classic horse stories as *King of the Wind*; *Misty of Chincoteague*; *Justin Morgan Had a Horse*; *Stormy, Misty's Foal*; *Misty's Twilight*; and *Album of Horses*, among many other titles.

Learn more about the world of Marguerite Henry at www.MistyofChincoteague.org.

Don't miss the
next book in the series!

Book 6: *True Riders*

Saddle up for a new world of classic horse tales!

For a full round-up of pony stories inspired by Marguerite Henry's *Misty of Chincoteague* visit **PoniesOfChincoteague.com**!